# AN
# OPEN
# PRISON

# AN
# OPEN
# PRISON

## J. I. M. STEWART

W • W • NORTON & COMPANY

NEW YORK     LONDON

First Edition

Library of Congress Cataloging in Publication Data
Stewart, J. I. M. (John Innes Mackintosh), 1906-
   An open prison.
   I. Title.
PR6037.T4660615   1984      823'.912      84-1687

ISBN 0-393-01861-X

W. W. Norton & Company, Inc., 500 Fifth Avenue, New York, N.Y. 10110
W. W. Norton & Company Ltd., 37 Great Russell Street, London WC1B 3NU

1 2 3 4 5 6 7 8 9 0

# AN
# OPEN
# PRISON

# I

I HAD SPENT eight months in America, most of them teaching on an exchange basis at a preparatory school in Vermont. Not that there had been any individual exchange involved. Nobody had come from Vermont to Helmingham, since my job had been taken over by somebody on the spot: a retired colleague who was delighted to get into harness again. I had been under an 'exchange' system only as having been one of a group scattered around the United States, and roughly equivalent to a group of Americans scattered about England for something like the same period of time. I may say I had been rather surprised that Helmingham let me go so easily, since long leave is generally not thought to be consistent with the responsibilities of a housemaster. But our Head had very handsomely backed the proposal from the start. All seemed to have gone well, and I had no vain disposition to suppose that any of my boys had suffered from the interlude. I had enjoyed my travels, and when I did get back to Helmingham just before the beginning of a new term it was contentedly enough. I didn't even quail when, upon reentering my study for the first time, I saw a pile of letters waiting for me on the desk.

But then there was a knock on the door I had barely closed behind me. I called out *Avanti!*—not as expecting some intending Italian parent about to declare himself, but because schoolmasters do tend to institutionalize that sort of small joke, although only of course with their pupils. And I somehow knew that this was one of them: an early arrival by a clear day before the beginning of term. There are boys—destined to turn out sane and blameless citizens—who are so besotted by the place that they occasionally behave in this tiresome way. But I'd not have expected it of Robin Hayes. And it was Robin Hayes who now came into the room.

7

'Hallo, Robin! Stout of you to clock in early like this.'

It was odd how, during those American months, I had let the affairs of the House drop clean out of mind. Now I had remembered just in time that Hayes was behaving quite properly in arriving early and seeking to confer with me. He was a good all-round boy who had taken his Oxbridge hurdle early and gained a place at a decent college. With this settled, he had elected to return to school and receive due promotion to the position of Head of the House, thereby helping me through what he was pleased to believe would prove rather a sticky term.

So much I had gathered from a brief letter—not much more than a note—which I had received from the Head Master some weeks before. As I read it I could almost hear Hayes explaining his virtuous intention to the small group of dons interviewing him in Oxford. A minority of them would indulgently approve; the majority, while keeping mum, would believe the boy would do better filling petrol-tanks in the forecourt of a garage, or otherwise seeing something of the Real World before settling down amid the Dreaming Spires.

'Can I speak to you, sir?'

'Of course you can. Sit down.' I think because obscurely alerted, I said this in a no-fuss way. I even reached for a pipe from the pipe-rack which hangs on the wall beneath a yellowing group-photograph of boys ranged around one of my pre-decessors some time before the First World War. One hesitates, during one's mere ten or fifteen years' tenure as a house-master, to take liberties even with gruesome objects of that sort.

'I don't think it's going to be too bad,' I said. 'This term, I mean.'

But I could see already there was something wrong. Robin Hayes was an agreeable lad to have in the front row of a form, being alert and cheerful, and owning a clear complexion and a straight glance. But now he looked strained and almost ill. I braced myself for the term's first crisis, small or moderately large, to be decanted on me.

'I can see you haven't heard, sir. It's my father. They've put him in prison. Two months ago. Just at the start of the holidays.'

There had perhaps been the ghost of a reproach at the end of Hayes's speech, and a second's silence had served to make it almost audible. I regretted my habit when abroad of not regularly seeking out an English newspaper. For a good many weeks this boy had been expecting some sort of supportive letter from me. That seemed obvious. So I must try my best to be supportive now, and to make it clear that my attitude would also be the attitude of the entire reassembled House.

'Robin,' I said, 'I'm deeply sorry. What has it all been about?'

'I almost can't bear to tell you.'

'Whatever it is, I'm afraid you'll have to bear a good deal more than a frank and reasonable talk with your housemaster.'

'Yes, of course.' For a moment the boy eyed me curiously askance. 'Facing up. Squaring shoulders. All that.' He paused for a moment. 'You can't have heard a word,' he said. 'It's having been so petty and squalid that's so frightful. My father hasn't murdered the Dean's wife, or been caught seducing the Bishop's boot-boy. It has just been his fingers in the cathedral till.'

'Embezzlement?'

'Yes. And probably, among other things, to pay my bills at this school for the sons of gentlemen. What a laugh!'

'Robin, one of the difficulties will be not dramatizing things. Managing to think twice before producing the hard sardonic quip.'

'Sorry, sir.'

It occurs to me now that this was almost the last private occasion upon which Robin Hayes was to 'sir' me. 'Sir' from a senior boy to a master can be a stiffly distancing syllable—or so I had sometimes judged it in the past. So I don't suppose I minded young Hayes dropping it. His family situation was no doubt accelerating the maturing process normally operative at eighteen. Soon, whether warped or not by this sudden disaster, Hayes would be grown up.

But I wasn't at the moment making a mental note of that sort. I was recalling whatever I knew about the Hayes family. Hayes's father was not, as the boy's words might have suggested, himself a parson. But he was the leading solicitor in a cathedral city, and probably looked after the Chapter's business affairs. So his misdeed, whatever had been its scale, could virtually be viewed as a pilfering from the alms box. I could hear some decently saddened judge feeling constrained to make the point as he handed out his sentence. Hayes's mother, I happened to know, was a magistrate of the kind that gives quite a lot of time to sitting on the bench. There must have been accounts of all this in the newspapers I hadn't seen.

'You've met my parents,' Hayes was saying. 'When I first came here as a brat, and several times since. They sometimes said I was lucky to have you as a housemaster.' The boy stopped short on this, as if he'd spoken out of turn. I saw what he was thinking. His father was no longer entitled to be put on record as approving of me.

'Yes, of course,' I said. 'I remember them both very well.' For a moment I was at a loss—which is why an odd impulse of curiosity prompted my next question. 'What do they make your father—I mean how is your father's time occupied in prison?'

'He works in the garden. It's what they call an open prison. That's something of a contradiction in terms, isn't it?'

'It is, indeed.' The point, I felt, was a proper one for a well-educated boy to make.

'There are several other men, but it seems my father is the directing intelligence. And a first exhibit of his has just won a prize at a local flower-show.'

I'd have been obtuse not to feel something uncomfortable about this. It opened up the whole question of how the boy now regarded his father. So I went off on another tack.

'Had your mother known all the time . . .?' Too late again, I caught myself up. 'Has it been a great shock to your mother?' I emended lamely—and told myself I must do better than this.

'My mother's—well, showing the flag. She has the carriage, of course.'

'The carriage?' Hayes seemed to have made an extraordinary statement; I had a momentary picture of Mrs Hayes as a Victorian lady driven out to take the air.

'Or the posture or the deportment. I don't quite know what to call it.'

'The bearing?'

'That's it. Every afternoon she dresses up just a little more than—well, before it happened. She puts on a hat—that sort of thing. Then she walks through the Close and up the length of the High Street. Looking straight ahead and taking care to be acknowledged by nobody. Then she buys something in a shop and walks home again. I don't know whether it should be called pride. Anyway, it takes guts. And then I see my father.'

'You see . . .?' I was bewildered.

'I see *him* as he'll walk, if he ever does, up that beastly street—when they let him out again. A kind of furtive shuffle, as if he'd been inside for far longer that in fact he will be. The judge said something about the disgrace alone being a heavy punishment for one in my father's position. But then something about betraying an honourable profession. You know the way a chap perched up like that feels he has to talk. As a matter of fact, he has a grandson here.'

'Not in the House?' At this point I must have betrayed something like alarm, for an odd look of amusement flitted for a moment over Hayes's face.

'No, not as bad as that.' The tone of this reply hovered, I felt, on the indulgent. 'The brat's in School House. David Daviot by name. It's an additional irony. If that's the word.'

'But it isn't. *Eironeia* in Greek regularly carries a connotation of ignorance, whether actual or affected.'

There was a longer silence this time. Not unreasonably, Hayes seemed disinclined to say anything further until I had produced something more relevant than pedagogy. I wondered whether he had made a fairly long journey simply to tell me face to face that because of what had happened he was thinking better of his plan to return for a term or a couple of terms as Head of House. It was a problem on which I found myself unready to make a pronouncement off the cuff. I didn't myself want to lose the lad. But that was irrelevant to the decision he had to make. Money, it occurred to me, might be a consideration in his mind. I didn't know whether his term's fees had, as was the general rule, been paid in advance. If so, and if Hayes now withdrew, the school bursar would in the circumstances certainly send the money back. But to whose benefit, heaven knew. Perhaps to the disgraced Mr Hayes in his penal garden. Or perhaps to the defrauded Cathedral Chapter. There was a headache even here.

Meanwhile something positive had to be said, and it would be rash to proceed as with an open mind, exploring pros and cons. To do so might be to give the boy the impression that I was manoeuvring towards ditching him. And to that, it now came to me, I was wholly opposed. Here at school I was by law *in loco parentis* to Robin Hayes. And the circumstances of the case even pointed at me as being *in loco patris* in particular. Hayes might of course have grandfathers, uncles, and even big brothers too. I didn't know. But here was the boy—attractive in himself and to be compassionated in his situation—in my study, and with a new term starting next day. It was clear to me how I ought to go ahead.

'It's a sad business,' I said, 'and it's going to take a lot of adjusting to. You'll come through it all right, Robin, unless I'm much mistaken in you. But it's a good thing, perhaps, that over the next twelve weeks your hands are going to be pretty full.'

'I do want to come back, you see.' Hayes said this cautiously and almost warily—as if afraid, I felt, of betraying too much sentiment about the House and about the school in general. 'Unless,' he went on quickly, 'you think it quite wrong.'

'I certainly don't think that.'

'But there's my mother obviously, and perhaps I ought to stick to her. Only I have a sister, two years older than I am, who has a secretarial job in the town, and who still lives at home.' Hayes was now speaking more quickly still. 'And my mother has always been closer to her than to me. One of those family things. And my mother doesn't want me to be held up. That's her expression. She means my plans and career and all that rot to go ahead just as if it hadn't happened.' Hayes paused on this, as if something new had come to him. 'Or because it *has* happened. The honourable task of redeeming the family name. It sounds a bit corny, I suppose. But I rather stay with the underlying idea. What do you think?'

I thought that the boy was showing up well, but knew that he wouldn't thank me for telling him so.

'My first useful thought is that you get down to the job here right away. Do a lot of the reading your future tutors have no doubt recommended to you. But also help me run this unruly menagerie of ours.'

'That's just what I don't want to do: the whole prefectorial business.' Hayes's face had flushed suddenly, so that I saw we were coming to what he felt to be the crisis of our discussion. 'There's a tiptop Head of House waiting in Macleod. I just want to retire into private life as a respectable Senior. To be unobtrusive. Just an observer.'

'Absolutely impossible.' Perhaps for the first time in this difficult interview, I spoke with full conviction—this even although I felt that the boy's mind was not entirely open to me. I thought of Mrs Hayes in that High Street: very much a person observed rather than an observer. Perhaps the boy felt that in that rôle he himself could no longer tolerate scrutiny. But whatever was nebulously in his head, I had to come down on it at once. 'Everybody knows you're due to be Head of House, Robin. So you'd be contriving a piece of theatrical nonsense, and everybody would be outraged. Morale would disintegrate, and the Head Man would just sail in and expel both of us.'

'I wouldn't like that.' The boy had contrived to raise rather a cautious smile at this perhaps unseasonable extravagance. 'And I don't know about morale. But I do know that it's a wholly moral authority that a Head of House has to be able to exercise. We're a civilized school, and prefects oughtn't to go round lamming into brats' bottoms with a cane to get a perverted sexual gratification out of it.'

'As they did when I was your age, Robin.' I had been surprised at the vehemence of that last speech, which hadn't been pitched at a customary master-and-boy level. I tried to recall whether Robin Hayes had come to us from a prep school in which there were archaic goings-on. But now I had to stick to the main point. 'Robin, listen. Everybody in the House will come to know about your father, and they'll all back you up like mad. And it will be the same when you arrive in that Oxford college. Neither what you call your moral authority nor just your general agreeableness will be thought of as in the least impaired by anything that has happened in your home. I sometimes think that the only good point about public-school boys and undergraduates in a college is their astonishing loyalty within the gang. No doubt it applies to skinheads and punk rockers too. And now go away and jump to it. My notice appointing you will be on the board within the next ten minutes, and then you can put one up yourself right away. About stacking tuck-boxes in the locker room, or anything of the sort that you please. And come in to supper with me at about half past seven, and we'll talk about other things.'

'Very well.' Hayes had got to his feet, and the slightly equivocal smile made another brief appearance. 'I'll do just as you tell me. Provisionally, that is.'

'Yes, of course. You're not signing indentures, you know.'

'I think you have a bit of a line on that loyalty biznai yourself. Half-past seven, then.'

And the boy departed. For a moment I wondered about the odd word he'd used—and then I remembered it belonged to Beetle's slang in *Stalky & Co*. It was clear that Hayes felt very miserable about his father's disgrace. That he could manage a momentary and friendly mockery of his housemaster doing his thing seemed not a bad augury for the coming term.

So I was left alone and to my own reflections. It was a situation in which I'd too rarely find myself during the three months ahead. An unmarried housemaster is regarded as *lusus naturae*, a freak unencumbered by private cares and therefore at all hours available to elucidate whatever professional conundrums turn up. It was true that I had an admirable Matron. Miss Sparrow, a lady of mature age, was adept at momentarily extending the reach of her authority so as to relieve me of much pointless badgering. And Miss Sparrow maintained, from term's end to term's end, a sensitive finger on the pulse of the House. I didn't feel I could properly repeat to her in any detail my talk with Robin Hayes. But what had happened to Robin Hayes's father was public property. I could discover what, in a general way, she felt was going to be the boy's position among us. Not that I hadn't—as must be clear from what I've written—made up my mind on how he was likely to be regarded by his schoolfellows. But it would be reassuring to have my own view confirmed by a good judge of boys' behaviour.

These thoughts—not of a robust order, I can now see—were in my head when suddenly they were displaced by a vivid visual image—almost an eidetic image such as comes to one on the fringes of sleep. What I thus saw was Mrs Hayes, walking up that High Street and wearing that hat. I could have described the cut of her clothes and named the colour of her scarf. She was a handsome woman in early middle-age, big-breasted but with the further bulk of her person well-controlled whether by regimen or by art. And there was no doubt about what her son had called her carriage. She moved as might an Italian woman indulging herself in the *passeggiata* while conscious that she belongs to the leading family in town. It was an apparition, I realized, compounded of memory equally with imagination: I must have seen Hayes's mother thus walking between chapel and cricket-field upon some parents' summer-term occasion.

But what then of Hayes's father? Was he too going to dredge himself out of memory—but in the broad-arrowed, pyjama-like garments in which convicts were invariably portrayed in the comic papers of my childhood?

Mr Hayes, I found at once, was eidetically a non-starter. I could summon up only a dim image of him that told me nothing—or perhaps only that *he* was dim. But yet again, he wasn't quite that to his son. 'Furtive shuffle' had been Robin's proleptic vision of how the wretched man would move when let out of gaol. It had been an uncomfortably evocative phrase. I didn't think, however, that one could take it as betraying that a settled resentment was now the main component in Hayes's feeling about his father. I'd rather have not heard it, all the same.

Embezzlement, I next told myself, is surely a pitiful kind of criminal enterprise, particularly when indulged in on a small scale in a county and cathedral town. Sooner or later one is almost sure to be detected—and without having enjoyed much fun meanwhile. The conjectural dimness of Mr Hayes chimed in with that clearly enough. And now another point occurred to me. There was nothing out of the way in a woman of some standing in a community being elevated into acting for it as a magistrate. But there was likely to be something masterful about such a person, all the same. And although Mr Hayes might have been too superior a solicitor to do much or even anything in the way of defending drunks and poachers and careless motorists before a batch of local beaks, there couldn't be other than some awkwardness in two diverse legal activities cohabiting under one roof.

And finally in this survey of the situation there was something else that Hayes had told me about his set-up at home. 'One of those family things' had been his comment on the fact that his mother inclined more to her daughter than to her son. I felt this to contribute to my view—a sketchy view—of the Hayes family as matriarchal in its structure. Ma Hayes—it might vulgarly be put—was boss. Several of my fellow housemasters, to whom the very idea of female dominance was abhorrent, believed that difficult or out-of-step boys often proved to have that sort of background.

Later that morning Miss Sparrow came in for what was our customary beginning-of-term review of the state of affairs on the domestic side of the House. I used to make a little joke with her about what I called our 'chronic anxieties over the cook'. Strictly speaking, I was as responsible for all that sort of thing as if I had been the sole proprietor of a lodging-house. But here again Miss Sparrow was well equipped to provide—as unobtrusively as might be—a welcome lending hand. Not that she was unobtrusive in a general way. An admiral's daughter, she would have done excellently in private theatricals as a jolly Jack Tar. There was something about this that made our relationship an easy one. It might readily, I suppose, have been delicate, since she was, after all, a single lady residing with a single gentleman under one roof. I was not wholly without masculine support from time to time, since I occasionally had a junior master quartered with me. But as my companion in the

House Miss Sparrow was at present as sole as the Arabian bird—although the comparison is no doubt inept, the phoenix having been of the male sex if of any sex at all.

I gave Miss Sparrow some account of my American experiences, and she responded with a brisk narrative of having accompanied an invalid brother to Crete and Rhodes. It had been a packaged tour, but one of a highly cultivated sort. The brother—not a retired sailor but a retiring Cambridge scholar—had been incensed by the insufficient archaeological learning exhibited by the Greek cicerone of the party, and had judged it necessary to set matters in a clearer light by delivering extemporary lectures of his own. The actual occasions of his doing this could not, I felt, have been other than embarrassing. But Miss Sparrow succeeded in making them sound quite funny.

We then got down to that domestic business, but it didn't occupy us for long. I could see that during my long absence things had ticked over very well. There were to be a dozen new boys, and they would arrive, some with parents, that afternoon. It was an arrangement giving these small fry the better part of a day to settle in before the confident and noisy established crew arrived. A running tea-party for dads and mums was entailed on me as a result. But here again Miss Sparrow had been at work, producing as a kind of *aide-mémoire* some jottings on those of the neophytes whose special needs I ought to show myself aware of. When we had run through these I turned to what was much more certainly in my mind.

'It seems to have been a bad business,' I said, 'that of Hayes's father.'

'Yes, indeed. Poor old Toad.'

'Toad?' I repeated. It seemed an odd way to refer to an unfortunate solicitor.

'Toad in *The Wind in the Willows*. He went dippy about motor-cars, too.'

'I'm afraid I don't catch on to this.'

'You didn't read about the trial?'

'I hadn't so much as heard of it until the boy came to see me earlier this morning. But what he had to say distressed me very much.'

'Then I'm sorry to have been flippant about it.' Miss Sparrow's sorrow was not reflected in her features, which never bore other than a cheerful cast. 'You see, it was the Rolls-Royce that took the public fancy, and led to a fairly full reporting of the whole case. Mr Hayes pleaded guilty to the charge, and was allowed by the judge to make a statement from the dock. He said he'd always wanted a Rolls-Royce, and was saving up for one. Unfortunately it had turned out that he was building up the necessary cash at the expense of other people.'

'Good heavens, Miss Sparrow, the wretched man must have been out of his mind! Wasn't his sanity inquired into?'

'Apparently not. The judge said something in passing about "reprehensible eccentricity", and left it like that. He probably felt that poor Mr Hayes had said the first thing that came into his head—by way of concealing, of course, some authentic reason for his misconduct. My own guess is that he was being blackmailed over something, and that the judge, a Mr Justice Daviot, took a humane view of the affair, and called it a day, so to speak, on the Rolls-Royce story.'

'It seems to me likely that your guess, my dear lady, will have been shared with a good many other people.'

I didn't, I ought to say, address Miss Sparrow as 'my dear lady' except when I was considerably upset. I may have been reflecting that there was something peculiarly unfortunate in the Hayes affair trailing behind it a suggestion of misdeeds still unrevealed. But I now produced a factual question which I had somehow been unable to put to the imprisoned man's son.

'For how long was Hayes sent to gaol?'

'For two years. I believe that means in practice sixteen months. But only if Mr Hayes behaves in a well-conducted way.'

'And it means that Robin Hayes will be in his first year at Oxford. The whole thing, Miss Sparrow, is the devil of a mess.' I paused on this, recalling that Robin Hayes had said nothing to me about the Rolls-Royce, which he probably regarded as an unbearable absurdity. Then I remembered something else. 'It seems there's a boy called Daviot in School House. A brat, as they insist on going on calling juniors. A grandson of this judge. Do you happen to have heard of him?'

18

'I believe I've noticed the name in the school roll. The connection didn't occur to me. And it seems not likely to add to that devil of a mess.'

Had Miss Sparrow and myself not been fast friends, this echoing of my phrase might have been irritating. As it was, it was merely being hinted to me that we mustn't make too heavy weather of the Hayes affair. Nevertheless, I instanced a further misgiving.

'It's curious,' I said, 'how in a public school each house tends so much to keep itself to itself. Wholesome rivalry at a distance, and so on, is the key to our relationships. So I don't think there will be silly gossip about this unfortunate business throughout the school. Only I wish the Daviot boy were a little more senior than he is. Some of my colleagues moan over the difficulty of having to cope with young men within a system essentially designed for children. My own view is that it is often the younger boys who are irresponsible. They haven't quite got hold of the spirit of the place.'

Miss Sparrow might well have made fun of this school-masterly remark. Instead, she looked serious, and made a thoughtful pause before speaking again.

'I heard that Robin Hayes had gained a place at Oxford. That makes his time his own for a good many months ahead. Has he had any reason to come back to school?'

'I have the impression that he planned it out quite long ago. He'd have a shot at Oxford entrance, and if he made it he'd return to lend a hand with the House.'

'I've known of boys doing that from time to time. It's usually because they want a spell of power before becoming insignificant freshmen at a university. But I'm not sure that anything of the kind quite fits in with my idea of Hayes.'

'It doesn't any longer seem to fit in with his own idea of himself either.' I believe I betrayed some annoyance as I said this. 'He wanted to return as a private citizen. That makes nonsense of his notion of being my right-hand boy. I had to tell him it wouldn't do.'

'No doubt you were entitled to do that.' When minded to, Miss Sparrow never spared me a hint of criticism. 'But I continue to find the whole thing puzzling in the light of his present fix. For it *is* a fix. And I'd suppose it would be his impulse to get away from the old familiar faces, not to dive in among them.'

I felt that there was more force in this contention of our Matron's than I was altogether willing to acknowledge, and I hesitated to reply with any reference to what Hayes himself had called the loyalty biznai. So I thought of something else.

'It's a good point,' I said. 'But look at it another way. The boy suffers this terrific shock about his father, and feels that a whole alien world is staring at him in that gossiping cathedral town. But here at Helmingham is a society in which his own efforts have gained him a secure and decent regard. From you and me, Miss Sparrow, as well as from his peers. He has a place here, and he makes for it. In your own phrase, he dives in among us. We mustn't let him drown.'

Perhaps I meant to say, 'let him down', since I am not much given to metaphorical expression. But Miss Sparrow seemed to judge that I had designed to close our conference on a note of muted drama. So she went about her business as I did about mine.

For a minute or two I wasn't quite sure what my business was. At any time the beginning of a new term brings a housemaster innumerable chores, and this increases—at least the sense of it increases—if one has had a spell away from the school. There was that pile of letters. But then it occurred to me that the proper thing would be to make a species of courtesy call on the Head Master. I had been away for quite a long time. So I crossed the cricket field to John Stafford's house.

Stafford had a 'come in at any time' rule with members of the staff. He worked with his study door open, and one either walked in with a token knock or halted at any sound of voices and hung about or went away. On this occasion he was disengaged, and he stood up at once and shook hands.

'Delighted to see you back, Syson,' he said. 'I hope you're feeling refreshed.' The tone of this was correct, but I didn't quite like the choice of words. Conversing with Stafford, one frequently didn't know whether he had been inadvertently tactless or deliberately astringent. And here there seemed to be an intimation that I had been judged to leave Helmingham in a jaded and probably rather useless state. 'You must be particularly glad to find,' Stafford went on, 'that things have been going unusually well on the classical side.'

Spoken thus to the head of the school's Classics department, these words were infelicitous, to say the least. But Stafford was being hospitable the while, having moved over to a side table on which stood half a dozen wine glasses and a single decanter. The idea was, I think, to suggest to parents that none of us at Helmingham was of a heavily bibulous habit.

'A glass of sherry, Syson?' he asked.

I accepted sherry. Stafford always addressed us by our surnames. And we always replied, even upon the most informal occasions, with 'Head Master'. I approved of this. Between adults, one ought not to address as 'Rupert' or 'Roger' a man who cannot reply comfortably with 'Timothy' or whatever it may be. And to have the junior masters saying 'John' to Stafford would have been inappropriate.

'Thank you for your note about Hayes,' I said. It was an index of how keenly I felt for my boy's position that I started in with this at once, and before there was any chance of small talk about my travels.

'Hayes?' For a moment Stafford appeared to be at sea, as if effort were required to disentangle this particular boy from amid the multiplicity of his headmasterly concerns.

I was annoyed by this, as I judged it, affectation—which accounts for what I next said.

'It was perhaps, Head Master, a little on the uninformative side.'

'My dear Syson, I'm extremely sorry. Deeply sorry.' Stafford was inclined to be lavish with his purely formal expressions of contrition. 'I hesitated to burden you with the boy's troubles until you were back at school. And I corresponded, I hope adequately, with his mother. No doubt she has written to you as well.'

'No doubt. The letters that came too late to forward to me are waiting for me in my study now.'

'I can see that Mrs Hayes is worried about the money—both in relation to us and to Oxford later on. Of course the boy has been rather brisk about Oxford under their present early-place system. I'd have preferred him to wait a bit and go after at least a minor award. He's very fair exhibitioner standard, I'd say—and as the family fortunes have turned out the money would probably be useful. Not that in cash terms open scholarships and exhibitions are of much account nowadays, as you know.'

'Certainly I do. And I fear the Hayeses' finances may just be at a tricky level for getting any decent grant from the public purse. I suppose, Head Master, we might find something ourselves to help the boy through.'

'My dear Syson, anything of the kind that you proposed would certainly be approved at once. Of course, inquiries would have to be made. It's conceivable that there are affluent relations not too far away.'

'As a solicitor the lad's father is presumably a gonner for good.'

'I fear so. The Law Society tries to be lenient when such disasters come along. When a man loses first his liberty and then his job there is an uncomfortable sense of double penalty about the thing. But you can't get round embezzlement. The poor devil will be struck off for keeps. Another glass?'

I declined this invitation, but took it as a hint that enough had now been said about Robin Hayes and his misfortune. At the same time I remembered that two or three men whom I had met in America had charged me with messages of regard to John Stafford. That species of second-hand cordiality more often than not slips my mind, but I was glad to be explicit about it on the present occasion. It would serve to wind up this not particularly necessary call on the Head Man. (It was thus that we referred to John Stafford among ourselves and occasionally to the older boys.)

So I delivered the messages I had been charged with, and Stafford with his customary conventional politeness offered an appreciative word or two about each of the senders. I then got up to take my leave. But Robin Hayes still ran in my head, and I paused at the door to say another word about him.

'There's one further thing about young Hayes, Head Master. It's something he told me—although without seeming to be at all concerned. It seems that the judge who tried his father has a grandson now in School House.'

'Ah, yes—a junior boy called Daviot. His parents are dead, and he is his grandfather's ward. Both boys were at Birnam Wood.'

'Birnam Wood?' For a moment I really thought that I had been offered some arcane reference to *Macbeth*. Then I remembered that this was the sufficiently unlikely name of quite a well-known prep school. Robin Hayes's prep school, in fact.

'Both Hayes and Daviot?' I asked. 'They can't have been contemporaries there.'

'Obviously not. But they did overlap. Hayes was in his last year there when this Daviot child was in his first.'

At this moment the Head Master's telephone rang, and he turned to the instrument with a resigned gesture to me which concluded our interview in a gracefully informal manner. So I walked back to the House. As I did so, I tried to recall just what Robin Hayes had told me about David Daviot. He had certainly said nothing about a prep school. But his attitude to the judge's grandson had been fairly casual, and there was no reason why he should have said more than he did. Probably what he had not very accurately called an irony did irk him more than he cared to acknowledge, and he had wanted to say nothing more about it.

As I returned to the House I was made aware of various evidences that the new term was now advancing upon us rapidly. From several vans 'luggage in advance' was being distributed higgledy-piggledy in front of one house or another— and with an uncertain accuracy which was occasioning the customary rude exchanges between the railway people and the school porters. Refrigerated vehicles were delivering in a more orderly fashion a routine consignment of the endless provisioning required for some six hundred hungry (and often unreasonably fastidious) boys. On the playing-fields several men perched on ladders were giving goal-posts a belated lick of paint.

23

I made no pause to inspect any of these activities, being curious to discover whether Robin Hayes's mother had indeed written to me, and if so to what effect. I was habituated to going rapidly through a fairly substantial batch of mail, since boarding-houses at an English public school seldom run to a secretary, and had certainly never done so in my own case. So I separated out the envelopes clearly suggesting private correspondence. The third of these, when opened, proved indeed to be from Mrs Hayes.

Dear Mr Syson,
    You will by now have heard of my husband's misguided conduct. My daughter and son must not be affected by it in any way. My husband's absence will be of less than two years' duration. This is a common enough period of separation within families: for example, when a father or son is on a tour of duty overseas. I do not propose therefore that my children visit their father in his present situation. But I myself have done so, and may do so again if family business requires it. I found him much (and I judge needlessly) concerned about Robin's immediate future. I myself see no reason why, when Robin goes on to Oxford, he should not read Law: it is what I have intended from the first as a preliminary to his being called to the bar. Will you be so kind as yourself to visit my husband, and set the matter in a proper light. You simply write to the governor of Hutton Green, who will arrange a time.
                                    Yours sincerely,
                                    EDITHA HAYES

My first response on reading this letter was one of displeasure before its deplorable tone. Merely regarded as an effort at prose composition, it conveyed a curiously bleak effect. But neither with that, I saw at once, nor with the specific concluding infelicity of her manner of laying an injunction upon me, had I any concern. The woman's husband was in prison; if she had been thrown off balance there was nothing surprising in the fact; it would be wrong in me to stand on my dignity and turn her

24

proposal down. It could not but be to the advantage of her son that I should discuss his affairs with his father, whether in prison or out of it. So I wrote a reply at once.

Dear Mrs Hayes,

Thank you for your letter. I had a talk with Robin this morning, immediately after his return to school. He is now Head of House: my head prefect, that is to say, and as a consequence a school prefect as well. I am very pleased he has returned to us.

I will make at once the arrangement you suggest for a meeting with Mr Hayes. Here I would remark only, and as a generally held academic opinion, that reading Law at Oxford is not in all cases the best preparation for entering upon a barrister's career.

Yours sincerely,
ROBERT SYSON

Having sent off my letter, I went to the telephone and drummed up an unattached junior colleague I had noticed about the place to come to an evening meal with me. Robin Hayes, I guessed, would be relieved that he wasn't going to have an immediate further tête-à-tête with his housemaster.

## II

I DROVE OVER on my mission to Mr Hayes some ten days later. All that my Ordnance Survey map showed me was a Hutton Park, near the middle of which stood a mansion-house named as Hutton Hall. I had no difficulty in locating it. Although in part screened by trees, its general character became apparent at about half a mile's distance as I reached the crest of a ridge of high ground to the south of it. It was large but architecturally undistinguished, built perhaps for some up-and-coming person in the latter part of the nineteenth century. The building disappeared as I dropped downhill again. Presently I was driving through a straggling and nondescript village without arriving at any glimpse of Mr Hayes's involuntary residence of Hutton Green. On its further outskirts I passed on my left hand first the church and a comfortable-looking hotel, and then several hundred yards of low stone wall. I supposed that here could only be the boundary of Hutton Park, and was confirmed in this view on coming upon a carriage drive and a lodge: the drive flanked by stone pillars on which hung open gates, and the lodge apparently unoccupied. It was absurd that I was still entirely at sea. But I should certainly have continued to drive on had I not happened to spot, fixed to one of the pillars which was crowned by a prancing and heraldically improbable hippogriff, an unobtrusively conceived metal panel which read:

*H.M. PRISON*
*HUTTON GREEN*

Thus finding my search at an end, I backed and then ran up the drive. It went straight through the park between lines of beeches, and over a considerable area on either hand any scattered timber had been removed in the interest of athletic pursuits. To my right there lay a cricket field with its central area, sufficiently broad for three or four pitches, roped off to discourage undesirable out-of-season incursions; to my left was a somewhat undersized soccer ground, surrounded by what appeared to be a well-maintained running track. I concluded that the disgrace of Hutton Hall (for one describes as disgraced a large house fallen upon hard times) must have come about by stages, and that it had quite recently been a boys' private school before becoming a rural receptacle for the criminal classes.

I believe it was in some confusion of mind that I drew up before the front door. My instructions had been to give my name and ask for the Governor, but I recall that what my inward eye imagined with some vividness was being received by a seedy and depressed menial in threadbare and greasy black, who had declined with the house's decline from butler to general factotum around the place. Of course the door was opened by a warder. The man was certainly that—being dressed almost, but not quite, like a policeman. It is probably difficult for a normally constituted individual to undergo a first encounter with any species of professional gaoler without at least a small degree of irrational alarm. I managed to state my name and business, but retained little power of detailed observation until I was shown into some kind of waiting-room and left to myself.

What I was first aware of was a faint antiseptic smell, reminiscent of the boys' part of the House when it has had its thorough clean-through before the beginning of term. It was a small, bare room, with a bench and some uncomfortable-looking wooden chairs. On the walls were three or four group-photographs in which a man in civilian clothes, and with features that seemed curiously familiar to me, sat in the middle of one or another bevy of uniformed men all precisely resembling the warder—the 'screw', I suppose he might be called—who had admitted me. This, too, was disquieting. For some reason the thought came to me that the young Shelley (unlike Thomas Gray before him) had thought of Eton as a prison. This idle reflection was barely out of my head when I found myself ushered into the Governor's presence.

He was a man of about my own age. So much I saw at once.

27

He had been sitting behind a big and very tidy desk. But from this he jumped up the moment I entered the room.

'Pog!' he exclaimed. 'I was sure it must be you.'

How I came to be called Pog at Harrow I don't think I ever knew. All 'Pog' suggests is 'pug', and although not good-looking I certainly bore no resemblance to that particular breed of dog. Nicknames, moreover, were not much in vogue in my time. But 'Pog' it was—whereas Owen Marchmont had never been other than 'Marchmont' to intimates and mere form-fellows alike. The day on which public-school boys would address one another by Christian name (except on holidays spent together) still lay in the future. I made some reply to Marchmont's familiar greeting, and for moments we regarded one another with the compunction which attends suddenly recognizing before us what happens beneath the unimaginable touch of time. I then said what first came into my head.

'Why Hutton Green, Marchmont? It's not on the map as that.'

'I suppose because Hutton Hall or Hutton Park wouldn't sound quite right. Suggest elderly gentlefolk in a high-class sunset home. Not that we haven't got a few of them in residence. Listen.'

The morning was warm; there was an open window beside me; what I heard through it as I obeyed my old schoolfellow's injunction was a faint hollow click and then a further hollow click which could only proceed from one activity in the world.

'Croquet?' I said.

'Just that. They have quite a lot of free time, and all ages have to be catered for. By the way'—and Marchmont glanced at me sharply—'are you related to this chap you've come to visit?'

'Not remotely.' I hope I didn't say this as if repulsing an aspersion. 'I'm a housemaster at Helmingham, and Hayes has a son with me. Hayes wants a word with me about the boy. Or his wife says he does.'

'That woman frightens me, Syson. Turned up here as if she was doing the place a favour. Told me she was a magistrate. She gave me to understand—quite by the way—that she might pretty well turn in a report on me to the Home Secretary. I tried

28

to explain how we did our best with people like her husband. It didn't seem an angle on the affair she was much interested in.'

'Does Hayes play croquet?'

'I'd have to ask my Head Warder, who keeps the balls and mallets. But probably not. Hayes works in the gardens, and attends various classes from time to time.'

'Classes?'

'No end of them. And of course workshops as well. All tucked away in a warren of hutments behind the house. Elements of Accountancy is the popular thing at the moment. Makes some of them feel they'll get away with it better next time. And the locksmith's shop is pretty well frequented too.'

There was a flavour of burlesque about this which made me feel that Owen Marchmont was a man not altogether at one with himself. This thought prompted me to an inquiry which would have been impudent except by a kind of unspoken appeal to the unregarding frankness licensed between schoolfellows.

'What brought you into this line of country, Marchmont?'

'Coming out of the army and looking around. And I'd read a bit about the theory and the history of the thing. Penology, that is. I thought something might be done; even that there was a climate of opinion growing up that might help that way. But, once in, one can't be spectacular. And the basic situation is quite intractable. Who was the chap said something about a robin redbreast in a cage?'

'Blake, I think. It puts all heaven in a rage.'

'Right. But I don't go with the poets much. Stone walls do not a prison make nor iron bars a cage. Bosh. They bloody well do. Even if you gild the iron bars no end. Harrow or a snot-school. There's never been a boy at either of them who hasn't had his weeks feeling that he'd swop for a desert island like a shot.'

I was shocked by this, and almost forced into silence. Yet something, I felt, I had to say.

'I can see,' I ventured hesitantly, 'that yours must be a job in which it's sometimes hard to fight disillusionment. But there must be another side to the picture. There must be occasions when—well, when a touch of the humane and compassionate makes all the difference.'

'Taking away a man's liberty is a staggering thing.' Marchmont seemed scarcely to have heard what I had said. 'But for thousands of years it has gone on to the enslavement of millions. And every one of them has felt, as the prison doors clanged behind him, that he is a man cast alone among animals. Not necessarily savage animals, as in an arena. Just nasty, smelly, skulking ones.'

'Yours seems to be rather a special sort of prison, Marchmont. But I suppose you speak from your experience of others as well. What about the old lags who go back to prison again and again? They can't have that cast-among-animals feeling.'

'They may feel something as bad. Who was the wench got working on Ulysses' other ranks?'

'Circe.'

'Turned them into swine, but had a line in manufacturing wild animals too. Right? Your old lags may feel they've had both treatments: into savage animals first, and then broken in for the circus of Pentonville or the Scrubs.'

I found all this interesting enough, although force rather than clarity seemed to be the main characteristic of Marchmont's mind. I felt, however, that my mission at Hutton Green was still bodefully before me, and that I'd like to get on with it.

'At least,' I said, 'this unfortunate solicitor has presumably not been turned into a porker. What are the conditions under which I see him? Will one of your men be present?' As I asked this question I didn't much concern myself about the answer. What I did feel anxious about was the possibility that the Governor himself would take it into his head to usher me into Hayes's presence. I saw such a procedure as obscurely embarrassing. But my mind was at once put at rest.

'One of my chaps listen or peep in? Lord, no! You're not likely to be passing Hayes a hack-saw or some powerful explosive, are you? The Head Warder will take you along to him, and you'll find there's a bell you can ring when you've had enough of one another. I hope you can stay to lunch with me?'

I declined this invitation, explaining that over the next couple of months my time would seldom be my own. Although I liked my rediscovered schoolfellow Owen Marchmont, I felt an impulse to get away from Hutton Green as quickly as I conscientiously could.

The Head Warder was an elderly man with a benevolent and sympathizing air. I suppose it is by relations that imprisoned persons are most commonly visited, and he probably imagined me to be Mr Hayes's elder brother. The room into which he showed me was that in which I had waited previously, and it was again empty.

'He'll be along in half a minute,' the Head Warder said soothingly. 'He's been in the garden, and probably feels he needs a wash and brush up.'

I had no doubt imagined a prison as a place in which the inmates are marched smartly up and down, or round in circles, by warders shouting 'left-right, left-right, left-I-say, left-I-say' in a commanding military manner. But it was clear that Hutton Green was conducted on other principles. I sat down, thanked the Head Warder as he left me, and composed myself to await Mr Hayes's leisure. I didn't feel I had much to say to him, and was inclined to doubt whether he really had much to say to me. I was here, I told myself, only because the luckless man's wife liked pushing people around. Or, for that matter, making them stay put. Her son was eighteen and her daughter was twenty, but she had written as if it were for her to determine—and in the most absolute manner—whether these adults should visit their father in prison or not. I didn't need myself to be a father to know that, in the present age, any such writ simply doesn't run. Letters from apologetic parents, confessing their inability to persuade Billy or Bobby to this or that, came to me at the rate of several every term. I was often constrained to dissimulate the embarrassing fact that I myself hadn't a good deal more influence over Bobby or Billy.

There were footsteps in the corridor. I found myself trying to decide—and then, with an instant shift of impulse, trying precisely *not* to decide—whether they suggested Robin Hayes's 'furtive shuffle'. The door started opening, came to a momentary stop, moved again. Mr Hayes had hesitated on the threshold of the depressing little room, and then summoned up

31

sufficient resolution to enter it. Or so I read that brief pause. He was now before me, and I rose hastily to my feet. I wondered whether to take the initiative in offering to shake hands. It was up to him, I thought, since after a queer fashion he was my host. But with a glimmering of good sense I did make the movement and accomplish the ritual. But now, and just as he had hesitated to face me, did I hesitate to face him. I didn't want to look him in the eye. But this meant looking at his clothes, and that I didn't want to do either. At Hutton Green were they put in some distinguishable prison uniform? I didn't want to know—and the result of this was that I ended up looking at the hand I had just taken. This provided me with one simple fact at least. Mr Hayes worked in those gardens quite a lot.

'Do sit down,' Mr Hayes said.

I had expected to converse with Robin Hayes's father through one of those overlapping armoured glass contraptions which confront one nowadays when one buys a railway ticket or cashes a cheque in a bank. I'd have found anything of the sort difficult. As it was, I judged it wasn't beyond me at least to make do.

'I've gathered from Mrs Hayes,' I said, 'that you'd like to discuss Robin's affairs, and I'm glad to have the opportunity. I can assure you, for a start, that he's doing well. His form work is very solid. And, outside that, he's being thoroughly useful to me as my Head of House.' I felt I couldn't say less than this, although in doing so I wasn't being entirely candid. There had been something elusive about the boy during the first week of term.

Mr Hayes was silent, so that I had to wonder what to say next. The man's expression, I felt, might afford me a cue, and for the first time I took a straight look at him. There was something meagre in his appearance, and in this he differed from his son, who was robust, if in a fine-boned way. This rendered the more striking the fact that facially there was a strong resemblance between man and boy. Yet what they shared couldn't be termed expressive in the sense of suggesting any sort of temperamental affinity. I didn't feel either that Mr Hayes would make a reliable prefect or that his son might not be trustworthy in small financial matters. It was just a physical correspondence, and little was to be gathered from it. But here was Mr Hayes still saying nothing, and all I could do was to add to the commendation of which I had just delivered myself.

'The boy works hard,' I said.

'He pushes hard.'

I didn't make much of this laconic statement, the tone of which was not laudatory.

'An unnecessary term, or two unnecessary terms, still at school. At over a thousand pounds a time. Oxford or nothing. And then nagging about that car. Hard as hard.'

It may be imagined that I listened to this, Mr Hayes's first speech, with astonishment. I recalled his son's making some light remark about school bills. And I recalled the Rolls-Royce.

'That car?' I repeated stupidly. 'A Rolls-Royce?'

'A Morgan—the equivalent thing, it seems, among the affluent young. Of course I *said* Rolls-Royce. I wasn't going to point at him in open court, you know. Poor callow little brute.'

I didn't know how to take this speech—or that I wanted to take it at all. So I tried to edge away from it.

'I can understand, Mr Hayes, that there may be difficulties about money. I believe the school . . .'

'He can get money out of his uncle—my wealthy brother-in-law. I never could, but Robin can. If his mother will let him, that is.'

'About Oxford, then.' I saw there was nothing for it but to take hold of the conversation as well as I could. 'About which Honour School Robin should read. Am I right in thinking you see him as likely to go to the bar?'

'His mother's notion. Nonsense!' Mr Hayes said this robustly. 'He isn't clever enough.'

'Robin is a very adequately able boy.'

'That may be. But even if you are a good deal more than that, you have to wait for years for your briefs. Of course he can be called, and then look round for some job having nothing to do with the courts, for which being a barrister is considered as some sort of subsidiary qualification. But money pouring away all the time.'

It seemed clear, and far from unaccountable, that financial considerations had become of paramount importance with Robin Hayes's father. I tried again.

'Then, Mr Hayes, have you any suggestion for the boy yourself?'

'I think he might try for the police. Or perhaps the prison service.' Mr Hayes gave me a swift glance, so that I wondered whether it amused him to see me for the moment dumbfounded. 'I must speak to the Governor about it,' he went on. 'A Harrovian, but a very decent fellow. I'm a Carthusian myself.'

I didn't like this at all—and chiefly because Mr Hayes didn't really like it either. It had been an uneasy kind of humour, and I was surprised at my not having recognized in him the instant he came into the room an uneasy man. It was, after all, what he ought to be. From the moment of his being convicted his position had become impossible, or had vanished. He had no place in society, nor ever would have again.

Such for a time was to be my feeling after my visit to Hutton Green. I can now see that it was wrong and also snobbish. Had Mr Hayes been a genuine gardener of the humble 'jobbing' sort; had such been his unassuming position in life; had he simply reached through a window and grabbed a wallet: in these circumstances my mind would have encountered no difficulty in thinking in terms of adequate expiation, of rehabilitation, of recovered self-respect, and the like. Mr Hayes's crime, one might say, had consisted in his having as a boy got himself sent to Charterhouse. *Noblesse oblige*—even the not very considerable *noblesse* that inheres in receiving an education among gentlemen. These were conventional reflections. At the same time I was puzzled by Mr Hayes, as if there were a side to him of which I was only obscurely aware—something unpredictable and not quite to be written off under the 'shabby scoundrel' formula.

But had my visit in the slightest way been any good? I decided that it had achieved nothing at all. As I had taken my leave of Mr Hayes I said a few words of the 'if anything happens I'll let you know' order. It was a familiar utterance with me on

34

concluding an interview with a parent, but it didn't sound convincing when offered to a felon. (Whether Mr Hayes was technically a felon, I wasn't sure. I had a notion one has to assault somebody to gain that status.) If I had come by anything it was a new, or augmented, view of Robin Hayes. His father had spoken disagreeably about him as a kind of family extortioner. In court he had protected his son—apparently by saying 'Rolls-Royce' when he should have said 'Morgan'. But to me he had virtually insinuated that it was the boy's demands which had prompted him to crime. This was horrible any way on; it could be felt as even more unsavoury than the suspicion I had shared with Miss Sparrow that Mr Hayes's dire need of money might have had its background in blackmail not in the least of a domestic order.

Yet I doubted whether Robin's conduct, even if it had been much as his father represented it to me, was justly to be viewed in a very unfavourable light. I reminded myself that at seventeen one can gain a licence and drive a car, and I knew that several of the boy's contemporaries owned cars at home, although they were of course not allowed to bring them to school. They were mostly the sons of business people with plenty of money around. Robin might have been insufficiently aware that his father's circumstances were very different. And of course there hadn't actually *been* either a Morgan or a Rolls-Royce— Mr Hayes having presumably been 'nicked' before any such purchase was made. Again, school agreeably continuing through one's nineteenth year, with Oxford or Cambridge to follow, was a taken-for-granted assumption by plenty of boys at Helmingham. All in all, it seemed to me that in an important point of character and family loyalty Robin Hayes deserved the benefit of any doubt. I was worried about him—or worried about him in a new way—all the same. It would be necessary to have a further private talk with him soon, since it was my duty to let him know that, at his mother's prompting, I had been to see his father. This would be an awkward occasion, but good might come of it. I hadn't seen much of the boy since his turning up on me the day before term began, and I felt that this was a matter of deliberate avoidance on his part. But ours was a situation in which misunderstandings could easily arise, so it was incumbent upon me to make it clear to him that I didn't regard him and his problems as a nuisance.

When I got back to the House I found that (as so often happened) a major crisis had erupted during my absence. Something had gone wrong with the gas supply in the kitchen; the boys had been obliged to put up with a cold dinner; and several of them had protested in a sadly underbred way.

# III

WHEN JOHN STAFFORD came to Helmingham—or rather
after he had spent a couple of terms playing himself in—he
instituted a number of sweeping changes. The most startling was
the placing of all extra-curricular activities upon a voluntary
basis. Military training was a partial exception: it could be
declined by boys who were prepared to 'do' something called
'Civic Duties' instead. Nobody much cared for these, which
consisted of such occupations as pushing old women around in
Bath-chairs, so in fact what was known as the C.C.F. went on
much as before. But among games boys were free, term by term,
to pick and choose—or they could decline anything of the sort
altogether. The majority of the staff (and I was among their
number) were aghast before this *ukase*. Housemasters in particular (rather comically, I suppose) simply felt that the end
had come; they were aware how a succession of hopelessly wet
days produces a sharp increase in disorderly behaviour, and even
costly damage to property, within a house. Eventually we were
most of us obliged to agree that the new scheme of things worked
well. This was particularly true of the oldest boys—the effective
management of whom had become more and more a matter of
insisting less and less upon their doing this or that. At first there
was a sharp turning away from team games (chiefly rugger and
cricket) to tennis, squash, fives, fencing, and similar activities
emphasizing individual encounter. But quite soon the traditional rivalry between house and house (as between school
and school) asserted itself anew, and nearly everybody was
playing football or cricket or hockey as before.

It chanced that on the afternoon of my return from Hutton
Green I came upon a boy called Iain Macleod standing before
the House notice-board, regarding with evident dissatisfaction a

list he had just pinned to it. Macleod, my second prefect, was the House's captain of rugger—worthily so, since he was the sort of full back who frequently scores tries himself and then converts them.

'Won't it do, Iain?' I asked humorously, having glanced not very attentively at what he was about.

'It will have to, I suppose. But just where am I to find my right-wing three-quarter, sir? Robin is as fast as anybody in the House, and he has such a safe pair of hands that by half-term he might be playing for the school. I was looking forward to nursing him for that. And for the House he just can't be replaced.'

'Good heavens, Iain! Has Robin gone on the sick list?'

'Nothing like that. He simply told me this morning that he has decided not to play rugger this term.'

I was upset. Being a prefect is a condition that imposes many responsibilities on a boy, and one of them is certainly playing rugger for his House if he is regarded as a key man in its side. John Stafford himself would have been the first to concur in this. It looked sadly as if Robin Hayes was going back on his implicit undertaking not, as he had expressed it, to retire into private life.

'But, Iain,' I said, 'surely you're not going to take that lying down? Haven't you reasoned with him—or threatened to have the whole team scrag him, if need be?'

'It wouldn't work, sir. And I didn't like to say too much. Not after what Robin told me. I expect you know what I mean.'

'Well, yes.' My heart sank before this. There had probably been no need for Hayes to 'tell', since by this time everybody must know about his father.

'Robin says he's determined to get over it.'

'I'm glad to hear that, Iain. Only . . .'

'He says that if he tries hard enough he's sure he can succeed by the end of term. Even get his hundred metres cert.'

'His . . .?' I found myself staring at Macleod stupidly. And he was looking strangely at me himself—having tumbled to the misunderstanding I had fallen into.

'It's a queer thing.' MacLeod went on hastily, 'in a chap so full of pluck as Robin. And he has a queer explanation. He says that when he was quite small his father used to chuck him into the sea and shout at him to save himself. His father believed that to be the best way to teach a boy to swim. It seems his father has a thing about swimming, and claims he got his half-blue at Oxford for water-polo. Can one get a half-blue for that?'

'My dear Iain, I've no idea.'

'It all sounds a bit phoney to me, anyway. One of those psychological things. You persuade yourself you have a memory of something that seems to be a rational explanation of something else. Really, it's a phobia—something quite irrational. There's a word for it, I gather. Hydrophobia. But isn't that a disease you get only if you're bitten by a mad dog?'

'In one sense—yes.' I found this confused thinking difficult to sort out. 'But I've certainly heard of people so unaccountably afraid of water that they panic if you take them on a pond in a dinghy. Rudyard Kipling was like that—and his father wasn't the kind of man who would chuck a child into the sea. I'd no idea Robin is inclined the same way, and has such a notion about it in his head. I just hope, Iain, that he isn't trying to go about this tackling the thing secretly. Haunting the swimming-pool when nobody else is around.'

'He couldn't do that.' Macleod said this so soothingly that I wondered whether the boys in general supposed that I was readily subject to fits of nervous agitation. 'The outdoor pool is drained this term, you know, and the indoor one is always locked up except when the bath-wallah is on the job. He gives a swarm of brats lessons four afternoons a week for the first half of term. And Robin says he's going to pocket his pride and muck in with the kids.'

'That's very sensible in him, no doubt.' I wasn't pleased, and I didn't conceal the fact. 'But everything in its place. It's a poor reason for cutting out of rugger. I'll have a word with him. Perhaps I can make him change his mind.'

'I'd rather you didn't.' Macleod, although junior to Hayes on the school roll, was the more mature young man of the two, and now he spoke with an assumption of growing equality between us, which I found entirely pleasing. I even asked myself whether it was for the worthiest qualities that I had made Hayes my top boy. Macleod was certain of a final term as Head of House, but if

Hayes hadn't returned to us he might have had a fair expectation of three. These seem insignificant or puerile matters to admit to a chronicle. But in a school they count for a good deal.

'I'll abide by your advice, Iain. I value it.' I spoke briskly, as if our conference had better now be closed. But Macleod had something further to say.

'Robin has told me about his father. I expect most people know about it, but I believe I'm the only boy Robin has chosen to mention it to. I don't suppose the situation is going to lead to any crisis. But if anything perplexing does come to your knowledge, sir, I hope you'll consider telling me. Robin Hayes and I are fairly close friends now.' Iain Macleod was an ugly boy with an engaging smile. And he smiled as he spoke. 'Or cancel "fairly",' he said. '"Chums", perhaps. Like the Boys of Greyfriars.'

I coped with this by giving an understanding nod as I turned away. Macleod hadn't, perhaps, reflected that I might receive confidences which I couldn't share with other people without having Hayes's permission.

As relevantly here as somewhere else, I may record that now and then an individual boy—that rather than a clump of them—used to occasion in me a pang I had come to recognize as arising from the fact of fatherhood having been denied me. Nor had I compensated for this, as some similarly circumstanced men do, by cultivating the power of making intimate friends— 'chums', if you like. What this casual encounter before the House notice-board left me with was an indefinable feeling, almost akin to envy or jealousy, as I thought of those two youths (for neither 'boys' nor 'men' is quite right) happily in harness together.

I am conscious of never having been too good with the junior boys. Athough without any memory of having been particularly unhappy at my own prep school, I have always regarded the English upper-class tradition of consigning children to a boarding-school at the age of eight or nine to be little short of barbarous. I don't feel the same about their arrival, probably at the age of thirteen, to face the rough and tumble of a large public school. Sometimes I am not quite happy with it, all the same. And it was one result of this that at Helmingham I commonly found it difficult to get on close and easy terms with the 'brats'. But here Miss Sparrow had been a great find. It is of course the recognized function of a matron in a boarding-house to mother the younger boys, and the responsibility is much increased if the housemaster is unmarried. The senior boys don't often make this type of identification; they would like a young and pretty matron to whom they could make experimental passes of—if there be such a thing—an entirely chaste sexual order.

Miss Sparrow held Sunday tea-parties which turned into cheerful romps four or five times a term. More importantly, she was the established confidante of every boy who sought one; to pass her room was commonly to be aware that she had a visitor and that the talk was of sisters and dogs and ponies—even of gerbils and guinea-pigs. But in this field of endeavour the older boys fell to me, and I cultivated for it such talent as I had. One of my habits was to take advantage of the free half-hour between the end of supervised prep and the House supper-hour. Sometimes two or three at a time, and sometimes individually, the fifth and sixth formers would be invited to drop in on me for a glass of wine and casual conversation. I recall with pleasure and some modest surprise how seldom these occasions turned sticky. I believe that here I owe a debt to my father who, throughout my later boyhood whenever I was at home, let few days pass without half an hour of useful and enjoyable conversation tête-à-tête.

It was of course proper that Robin Hayes should be early on my term's list for this occasion. And I had decided that as soon as he was sat down with his tot I would speak to him about my visit to his father. It wasn't a thing to come to casually or by the bye later on. So this I did.

'Robin,' I said, 'I called the other day on your father.'

I ought to have said 'I visited your father'. But Hayes appeared unconscious of this slightly awkward slip in idiom.

'Did he send for you?' he asked.

'No. The suggestion came from your mother.'

'Oh.' Hayes paused on this. 'But of course. She would.' He paused again. 'What did she have in mind?'

'Something I remember you mentioning yourself, Robin. She is concerned that your career should not be affected by what has happened, and she was anxious that I should discuss the problem with your father.'

'No problem. Or not of that kind.'

I found this clipped utterance disconcerting, and I paused in my turn to consider.

'About your being called to the bar,' I said.

'I don't intend to be called to the bar. I never have intended to be called to the bar. It has been just one of my mother's things. What did my father think?'

'He appeared to think that a lot of money would be involved. One has to wait a long time for one's first briefs, and so on. So he wasn't enthusiastic.'

'I'm glad to hear it. Not that the money is a real point.'

Hayes was silent after this. He appeared to feel that he had patted the ball back into my court. I felt discouraged. But if the boy was hardening in his contacts with authority in general I couldn't blame him over much. Nevertheless I became a little clipped myself.

'Not the point?' I repeated.

'I mean I've an uncle who will pay up if I ask him. My sister and I call him our wicked uncle. Uncle Jasper. With a name like that, and a reputation to match, you feel he ought to be a baronet.'

'Robin, please be sensible, and tell me about this uncle without being clever about him. Your father mentioned him. But is he really a factor in your situation?'

'I think so. Or I think he'd like to feel he is. Uncle Jasper believes he commands the subtle sort of flattery that goes down with a schoolboy.' Hayes glanced at me swiftly, and must have seen I wasn't very content with all this. 'He's an uncle on my mother's side,' he went on. 'I used to suppose that meant that my mother must have at least a little money of her own. Family money is usually a bit like that, isn't it? But it isn't so. Uncle Jasper *made* his money—which of course is less respectable than just inheriting it. He has bought my mother this or that from time to time, but in a general way he's pretty close-fisted. My father has had a go at him more than once, but all in vain. What made my father's applications awkward, I suppose, is that he disapproves of brother-in-law Jasper. On moral grounds.'

Robin was silent again, having achieved what he would no doubt call an irony. I told myself that every clever boy goes through a phase in which he has to talk for effect, and that the circumstances of my Head of House had precipitated him into it now, rather than—as was more usual—during a freshman year at the university.

'Let me get this clear, Robin,' I said. 'You feel that if money is needed to take you to Oxford, and then to launch you on a career in one profession or another, it would be reasonable for you to ask your uncle for it?'

'Reasonable, yes. But not perhaps very nice.'

I ought to have approved of this judgement, since it suggested a proper diffidence in sponging upon a relative. But there had been something faintly equivocal in Hayes's tone, and I felt a little at odds with him. I might have told him so had he not again taken charge of our conversation.

'Incidentally,' he said, 'Uncle Jasper is Jasper Tandem. The Tandem pop discs and cassettes. It's not very distinguished. But he got in, first on the one market and then on the other, bang on the ground floor. I don't think music means much to him. He's by way of despising what he peddles, and hasn't a clue that pop has its peaks as well as its swamps. My sister Julia and I believe he boxes clever in other fields as well. Clip-joints of a variously sleazy sort.' It amused some boys at that time to bespatter me with what they thought of as baffling slang. 'Well, that's my uncle, and I'm sorry I haven't made him sound very attractive, because I'm afraid he's going to ask to meet you quite soon. He's coming to Helmingham, he says, to see how I'm shaping up, and he'll take it for granted that you're going to be laid on.' Robin paused for a moment, and suddenly looked troubled. 'I'm sorry about all this,' he repeated. 'It's not what I should be talking about—or how, either. And I'm not sure I'm coping at all well with the House.'

I wasn't myself sure about this, and I reflected that a good senior prefect, although invaluable in a way, is prone to regard

43

himself as more of a linchpin than is necessarily the case, and to agonize accordingly. Robin (I was coming to think of him, as well as to address him, by his Christian name) had serious issues confronting him as a consequence of his father's turpitude, and a right or wrong resolution of them might reverberate through much of his adult life. I had thought of his duties as Head of House as a distraction from the unfortunate state of his home affairs. It hadn't been at all my idea that such vexatious (and, as the world might judge, absurd) employments as making small boys get under showers and big boys drink only their permitted half-pint of beer in what they were pleased to call their bistro should become a burden to my senior prefect. So now I said something cheerful about House matters, and avoided (as I think I had already decided to do anyway) all reference to the odd business of hydrophobia and swimming lessons. And then I came back to Mr Jasper Tandem.

'As for your uncle,' I said, 'it's true that I don't as a rule expect either aunts or uncles to turn up on me. But if Mr Tandem is likely to come forward with practical assistance to you in one form or another'—I thought this a judicious phrase to use—'then it will only be proper that he and I should get to know one another. Just give me reasonable notice, Robin, and I'll be delighted to meet him.'

'Thank you very much.' The boy stood up, and for an instant contrived to look at me still in a troubled fashion but somehow to a faintly amused effect as well. 'And thank you for the sherry,' he added correctly. As he turned and left the room, it was with a lightness and a curious economy of movement that might have been called graceful had the word been at all appropriate to a schoolboy. As it was, I reflected that here was a first-rate wing three-quarter likely to be lost to Helmingham.

I don't think I was much worried by this. My interest in games and in athletic matters generally was no greater than the conventions of my profession required. But I would be disturbed if the behaviour of my Head of House came to be judged by the school at large as eccentric or even 'soft'. And no sooner had this come into my mind than I caught myself wondering whether there might not be something in such a verdict. I liked Robin. Of that there was no doubt whatever. But it wasn't quite with the liking I felt from time to time for boys given vigorously to physical accomplishments and little else. I was becoming interested in what went on inside Robin's head. Yet wasn't this at least partly because of what had emerged about his family situation—and hadn't I once or twice speculated curiously on what might be the underlying relationship, and conceivable temperamental affinity, between the boy and his father? Mr Hayes's criminal behaviour had arisen, one had to suppose, from an inability to face up to his financial difficulties in a forthright fashion. Was it possible that his son owned a streak of the same weakness, and that he had invented the whole business of a fear of water, together with a sudden resolution to conquer it, as an easy means of avoiding the hazards and strains of attempting to become, by way of the rugger field, an idol of the whole school? And didn't this reading of his conduct cohere with the odd wish he had expressed to me at the beginning of the term 'to retire into private life'?

I am aware as I write that this string of questions must appear small-minded and gratuitous. Indeed, it is certainly so. I can only plead that among the vocational risks of schoolmastering is the growth of a habitual suspiciousness in face of the activities of the young. I don't know how it may be with girls, but boys delight not so much in deceit itself as in the skilful engendering of the imputation of it on grounds presently exposed as ludicrously fallacious.

However this may be, here I was, likening Robin's retreat upon a swarm of infants receiving swimming lessons to Achilles' legendary concealment among women. The thought was still in my head when, later that evening and while walking through the east cloister, I ran into Vass. Vass, a retired warrant officer of Marines, was the bath-wallah when teaching the junior boys to survive in water; more augustly, he presided over boxing, fencing, and Boats—Helmingham being in a modest way a rowing school. I judged Vass to be well met, and halted before him at once.

'Good evening, Mr Vass,' I said (for one should address a warrant officer like that). 'How are the juniors getting on with their swimming?' I asked this question in a casual and genial way, and was surprised by the long face with which Vass received it. And he spoke with corresponding gravity.

'As a matter of fact, sir, I was on my way up to see you. About Mr Hayes, it is.'

'Hayes?' I had been startled, but I don't suppose I showed it. 'I've heard he's taking lessons with you.'

'Yes, sir—along with the younger lads.'

'And he's getting on all right?'

'So it seemed, Mr Syson. So it seemed, although at times he was a little absent in his mind. Sitting on the edge of the pool and gazing at the small fry as if he didn't see them. I pulled him up sharp on it after a time. And he told me a funny thing.'

'Ah, yes.' I nodded as if with mild interest. 'That fear of water, eh?'

'Just so, sir. I used to hear of such a state often enough in the Service. It can be got over, and I told Mr Hayes he was right to try—but that he ought to have explained himself to me at the start. I was a bit sharp again.'

'Quite right, Mr Vass.'

'Well, the strange thing was there had never been a flicker of it, right from the first day of his getting into the pool. Nor after we'd had this word about it. So I was lulled, as you might say.'

'Something has happened?' I asked. I was alarmed.

'Yes—and very bad it might have been. I'd got him off the pole, and when I wasn't attending to him I let him plouter around with wings. Not that I approve of wings.'

'I understand they're no longer regarded as a good idea, Mr Vass.'

'Well, there was Mr Hayes—out of his depth as he oughtn't to have been. And suddenly he lost the wings. And panicked. Down he went, you know, and up with a mouthful of water, and flailing round, and down again. The regular thing. And I'd just taken it in when a smart little lad of the name of Barton, who hasn't all that more to learn, was in the water and after rescuing him. The best of the Under Fifteens, Master Barton is, and had been having lessons from me in emergency drill. He knew what to do and was doing it—prompt and without a mite of fuss. So I

46

held my hand while you could be counting ten. It might do Mr Hayes a bit of good, I reckoned, if he had to be hauled out of his trouble by a youngster like Master Barton.'

'There may have been something in that,' I said, not too graciously. Vass's Mistering and Mastering always annoyed me, although I knew that, oddly enough, it was one of his means of keeping the whole body of the boys in awe. 'But did you have to intervene?'

'That I did, sir—and I don't know when I last moved as quick as I did. For one moment it was all as it should be: Mr Hayes got on his back, and Master Barton beneath him, thumbs behind the ears and fingers to chin. And the next moment it was bloody hell let loose—begging your pardon, sir. Mr Hayes had been got well within his depth by the lad, so that there seemed no danger, nothing but what you might call an improper occasion, when suddenly the panic was on him again, and he was lashing around like a wild Irishman, and then his hands were round the lad's throat. It's the recognized risk, as you'll be aware, sir, in that situation, and I don't doubt Master Barton knew what to do. But he wouldn't have quite the right strength for the jab, you see, and in a flash there were the two of them, struggling beneath three feet of water. I had them out before anything you could call real damage was done—only there will be bruises on that game little chap's neck in the morning.'

'What about the other boys?' I asked. 'Were they frightened or inclined to make a sensation of it?'

'None of them was as frightened as me, Mr Syson. I doubt if they thought anything had been happening except the kind of skylarking I'm likely to take a gym-shoe to.'

I had never heard of this sanction as commanded by Vass, and it interested me.

'But you wouldn't,' I asked, 'take a gym-shoe to Hayes or any other senior boy?'

'Would I not, sir. The Captain of School himself would touch his toes if I told him to, and do his best to batter my nose in the next time we got in a ring together. It's a tradition, Mr Syson, a tradition of the school. I'm a regular old-style Master at Arms.'

As Vass had come to Helmingham some years after I had, it

seemed odd that I could be instructed about a streak of weird behaviour in the place after this fashion. I was perhaps the more struck by it because I had never myself hit a boy in my life. But this was to go off on a side-track, and I returned to the matter in hand.

'Were you coming across, Mr Vass, to consult me as to whether anything further should be done about it?'

'Only to report, sir. It's for you to say. So far as concerns Mr Hayes, that is. But perhaps I might say a word about him?'

'I'd be grateful if you would, Mr Vass.' I didn't say this out of politeness, for I was coming to feel that light on Robin Hayes might be prizeable from any quarter.

'Well, sir, I'd let be. Mr Hayes has what he must conquer if he's ever to look himself in the face, as you might say. There's not a doubt about that. And if you were to tell him he must give over, or even that he must switch to private instruction from me at such odd times as we could both fit in, it might upset him more than we'd care for. I've no thought to be curious, Mr Syson, but I gather that these days young Hayes has a good deal on his plate. So softly softly it had better be.'

I was struck by 'young Hayes', which seemed to signal a certain warmth of regard for Robin on Vass's part. I also took note that Robin's domestic difficulties had gained some currency among the lower hierarchies of the school.

'What about the boy Barton?' I asked. 'Is he likely to go chattering about this unfortunate affair to his admiring friends?'

'That he is not. I spoke to him.'

'Telling him not to?'

'Nothing of the kind, sir. Telling him he went wrong at an awkward moment, not getting that jab in, and that at life-saving he still has much to learn.'

'I see.' I was a good deal impressed by this command of a ruthless guile. 'And I agree with what you say, Mr Vass. I shan't discuss the episode with Hayes. He has his difficulties, we know. Of course the less they're talked about the better.'

I didn't really feel that the bath-wallah required or deserved a caution. It was simply that by now I was becoming jumpy over the whole Hayes affair.

*

But continuing my turn round the cloisters which form a prominent and disingenuous advertisement of Helmingham's antiquity, I realized that Vass's story had relieved me of an unworthy suspicion. Vass wasn't a man to be deceived by a boy in a swimming-pool, and it was clear that water held for Robin Hayes precisely that lurking power to terrify which he had confessed to his friend Macleod. His swimming lessons couldn't be a ruse for dodging the hazards of the rugger field—whether represented by painful injury or by the schoolboy's nightmare of playing for the school and dropping an easy pass at a critical moment in the game of the year. As for being unobtrusive and unobserved, it was true that swimming lessons undertaken amid a crowd of unregarded small boys could be conceived as an effective route to it. But not for Robin, since at any time his aquatic disability, if clearly exhibited and bruited abroad, would at least for a day or two have the whole school goggling at him. A head boy funking a dip! It would be quite something, that.

I found myself smiling as I thus reflected on the innocent anxieties of nonage. At the same time I was surprised by the lively character of the relief which the resolving of at least one aspect of the Hayes family imbroglio occasioned in me.

## IV

WITH A SINGLE exception, Helmingham's ten boarding-houses take their name from those of their first housemasters. My own house was Heynoe, and a portrait of Heynoe, a heavily bearded Victorian cleric, holds a place of honour in the boys' dining-room. Heynoe is the most recently established of the houses, and the school itself is in no sense an ancient foundation. It does not even represent, as do many of England's most famous public schools, the filching of a long-established school for poor boys and the turning of it into a school for rich ones. It was in fact started on quite a small scale in 1860 by a group of bishops, deans, archdeacons and laymen who were concerned over what they judged to be happening to the moral tone of public schools in general since the untimely decease of Dr Arnold of Rugby in 1842. There had been at that time only one boarding-house, and it was presided over by the Head Master himself. When other houses followed they took name in the manner I have described, but the pioneer establishment became known simply as School House. From that time forward, School House boys steadily maintained that theirs was a privileged position in relation to the school as a whole; that they in fact represented a kind of hereditary aristocracy entitled to the deferential regard of everybody else.

As may be imagined, this was not well received. The riposte of the other nine houses, much in evidence at house concerts and on athletic occasions, turned upon the circumstance that the school's pious founders had injudiciously exhibited their aspirations or apprehensions in too explicit a fashion in certain tags and apophthegms incised and gilded in the Gothic woodwork of the hall of School House. It is true that those which were not in Latin were in Greek. But every new boy in the nine later houses was obliged, at peril of penalties of a drastic sort which his immediate seniors were all too eager to inflict, to make himself sufficiently a classicist to be able to offer on demand a specious but ingeniously garbled translation of those noble exhortations and awful warnings—as, for example, when two resonant Greek words in the sixth book of the *Iliad* were turned into the injunction, 'Always be the little gentleman'. And just as street Arabs (as they used to be called) were believed to taunt one another with the question, 'How's your mother off for dripping?' so were School House boys prone to be solicitously asked for news of their own and their fellows' current moral tone. A good deal of inventiveness went to ringing the changes on what must sound rather a stupid amusement.

What of this is at the moment relevant to my narrative I can briefly explain. As with the boys so with the masters—at least during the fairly brief period with which I am concerned. School House was under a man called Taplow, an able fellow with a clever wife. He was our senior scientist, and before he had been with us long he had so made his mark in the school as to be quickly rewarded with a house. It was a rule-of-thumb and, as it turned out, not wholly judicious advancement, since Taplow was an easy-going man where the rigours of physics and chemistry were not concerned, and proved to be without much interest in watching over the everyday life of his boys. But he had reorganized and transformed the labs—securing for the purpose a bigger share of the school's financial resources than many of us quite approved. At the universities, however, the science dons were beginning to look out for Helmingham boys, and at the same time alert heads of prep schools were learning to steer those of their pupils given to maths and 'stinks' to harbour, if possible, in the supposedly superior intellectual milieu of School House. There is no question of how the rest of us felt about all this. Just as our boys spoke of 'the little gentlemen' of School House so did we, the other housemasters, speak of 'Taplow's young egg-heads'. We were decently proud of those boys when they carried off scholarships at Oxford or Cambridge, and I think there was a sense in which we liked Taplow well enough. But the underlying feeling was there, and since it affects my story I have to touch it

51

in. But I must not be misunderstood. Nothing approaching ill-feeling was involved. School stories used to make much of the conception of a 'cock house' as often in the minds of schoolboys, and School House, as I have implied, subscribed to the notion, although I don't think they used the term. Jocularly, we used to pretend to believe that it was quite urgently in the mind of Tim Taplow himself. We didn't, so far as I can remember, extend our facetiousness to the extent of adopting the 'moral tone' joke. There is much to be said for a good moral tone, and it is something that has come to be taken for granted in a modern public school. Occasionally, however, it is capable of vanishing—at least in some luckless single house—virtually overnight.

Going into our masters' common room for a cup of tea on an afternoon shortly after the episode of the swimming-pool, I found a debate going on between Taplow and a young man called Johncock. Johncock had joined the staff only in the previous school year, and was still, I believe, the junior man among us. He was a mathematician, but without the pre-dominant withdrawn quality that mathematicians commonly exhibit. There were always a number of assistant masters who had not been at public schools themselves, and he was one of them. John Stafford was keen on this mix of backgrounds—which was one of the policies (few in number) in which I was in accord with him. And Johncock was never slow to entertain us to expositions of his own point of view. It had been one of his earliest lines that on coming to Helmingham he felt as if he had tumbled straight into Noah's Ark. But quite soon he had abandoned this facile response to our days and ways for something rather more interesting. Cultivating the conversation of the most senior among us, he was building up what he called a symposium of views on how the life at English public schools ('private' schools, as he was fond of calling them) had been changing over the previous thirty or forty years.

The argument I had come upon must have taken wing from this territory; it was over the nature and causes of that earlier maturation (to my ear a somewhat barbarous word) which it was generally agreed that adolescent boys—and no doubt girls—in general exhibited.

'It's perfectly simple,' Taplow was saying. 'The little brutes have been better fed from the cradle onwards than any previous generations have been. And masses of antenatal care, postnatal care, decent standards of hygiene, and all the rest of it.'

'Won't wash,' Johncock said. 'Think of a hereditary aristocracy. Fat of the land all their days. But do they come on, emotionally or intellectually, faster than their less privileged contemporaries?'

'Yes,' somebody said, through a mouthful of cake. 'Certainly they do.'

'It's a matter of social assumptions,' Johncock continued, ignoring this. 'We've come to agree that you're grown up at eighteen and not twenty-one. That's because at eighteen a lad is fit to carry a gun, and get himself killed while trying to load it. And for some time before that he has himself been licensed to kill in a motor car or on a Honda or Suzuki or whatever. So it's only decent to give him a vote before he can tell a fool from a knave. Useless to expect him to remain in a place like this and behave like Tom Brown.'

'But they all do,' the cake man said. 'Just scratch any of them, and he's revealed as being as infantile as ever.'

'Sexual mores, too,' Johncock said, unregarding. 'Plugged at them on the telly from the age of about five onwards is the view that copulating is no end interesting. And all the rubbishing acquisitive attitudes thrown in. I'm all right, Jack. So bang goes continence, and all the pitiful junk about loyalty and fair play.'

'I'm not sure,' Taplow said, 'that this whole argy-bargy isn't based on a false premise.' Taplow was shifting his ground. 'Certainly in School House my young egg-heads, as you call them, sometimes seem to me to get younger every year. Take crazes. Crazes used to be a prep school phenomenon. You remember how it was. Quite suddenly every boy in the school playing conkers, or manufacturing a new sort of ink bomb, or being a Chinaman talking pidgin English. But now our own boys suffer such epidemics. It scarcely stops short of the sixth formers themselves.'

'There's a good deal in that,' I said—somehow prompted to intervene. 'Has any of you come across tummy-pummelling?'

'Yes,' Taplow said. 'I think it began in School House, and perhaps it has spread from there—as so much is said to do.'

'Wherever I go in Heynoe, there it is,' I pursued. 'Being carried on unblushingly.'

'Something with a sinister sexual significance?' Johncock asked.

'Nothing of the sort.' I was annoyed by this, which seemed uncalled for. 'My point is that it's a craze, and that it's among the most senior boys. One of them will be on his back with a bare belly. That's because a buckle or button might do mischief and spoil the act. And it *is* an act—quite an astonishing one. The boy tautens his belly muscles in some way, and another great hefty lad bashes a clenched fist, or two fists clenched together, down on this exposed victim. To no effect at all. But it's exclusively a senior boys' amusement. And it couldn't happen in a prep school, because young boys couldn't manage the necessary muscular control.'

'And tummy-pummelling,' Johncock asked, 'is something you go stumbling over as you do your prowling round?'

I hesitated to reply to a question thus rather offensively expressed. 'Prowling round' was a malicious travesty of one of my known habits. It had for some time seemed to me that I could no longer rely upon the traditional schoolboy's acceptance of the prefectorial system. Prefects were often regarded as spies— and this was the more true the more were old-fashioned (and to my mind brutal) sanctions denied them. So by keeping an open eye on things as I moved about the House I contrived to make it apparent that one or another turpitude had been detected by my own vigilance. But it thus became possible to represent me as doing too much fussing around, and this had been implied by Johncock. Taplow must have observed my discomfort, for he cut in with something else.

'What about dyed hair?' he asked. 'There's been enough of that for it to be called a craze. Robert, didn't I see a couple of Heynoe boys with green top-knots the other day?'

'I don't doubt you did,' I said. 'Two boys who are normally reasonable enough. When I asked them why they had done anything so senseless, one of them replied, "We're the New Jumblies, sir". It's hard to know how to cope with such nonsense.'

'How *did* you cope?' Johncock asked.

'I told them they weren't Jumblies but copy-cats, and that the working-class lads who daubed themselves like that were demonstrating against social deprivations which Helmingham boys ought to be thinking about.'

'Edifying,' Johncock said—humorously, this time, and without malice. 'But what did you *do*? What dread penalty did you impose?'

'An uncomfortable and rather futile scrub down by the school barber. I did add that if it happened again they'd go home. So they said, "Thank you, sir" in that stiff, offended way they command—and took themselves off like two animated gooseberry-bushes.'

'Good old Mister Chips!' Johncock said—outrageously, but without at all displeasing me. 'And now let's talk about the bug.'

'Which bug?' the cake man asked, turning round from cutting himself another slice. 'Place full of the things. Bugs, bugbears, and buggers. Not to speak of bugaboos.'

Nobody found this very funny. And Taplow, who owned a surprising skill with such moments, again spoke at once.

'Yes, of course. It's just during this term, and just in the crucial week of it, that the bug rears its ugly head. Will it strike again—and if so, in which house first? Usually it's School House, naturally. And then there's that customary spread. But School House stands to suffer most. That's a matter of statistics, so none of my colleagues will take offence at it.'

Taplow, whose sense of fun was very simple, laughed happily.

But the bug was no laughing matter. What was meant by it was one or another variety of epidemic illness such as afflicts most close communities from time to time. We know that in the Victorian period simple children's ailments—scarlet fever and the rest—were the terror of every nursery, since they were in fact

55

the Angels of Death to many infants. Boarding-schools seem to have been less afflicted, presumably because their populations had already been sifted through the operation of some Darwinian law. The modern boarding-school is affected in any grave sense hardly at all. Half a house, nevertheless, can go down with influenza or something of the sort within a week—and the week is always liable to be a disastrous one from an academic point of view. It may be the very week in which the senior boys are due to write their examination papers for university entrance—and if they have mumps instead nothing can be done about it. In remarking that School House stood to suffer most from any awkward coincidence of that sort Tim Taplow had been reminding us, as 'a matter of statistics', that he commonly had more than his fair share of clever boys on offer when these competitions came along.

Within days of that idle conversation in common room the bug had arrived—and its first abode, sure enough, was in School House. Two circumstances, however, made this something less than a calamity from Taplow's point of view. It was still early in the term, so that there was a good chance that the epidemic, whatever its nature, would have run its course well before that fateful week arrived. And this bug was—as Johncock expressed it—a choosey bug, with an apparently exclusive predilection for tender juvenals. In the context of the particular anxieties involved, brats could be regarded as virtually expendable. Let them be put to bed, glanced at now and then by the school doctor, and have their self-importance gratified by regalement with delicate broths and jellies. They could then be forgotten about. But their isolation from the all-important exam-confronting sixth formers must be absolute.

Taplow was unperturbed. He had coped with just this situation before. And indeed no seasoned schoolmaster agonizes over such matters. But it is otherwise with some of the boys—and not only those who see their smooth progress into a university as at hazard. Epidemics can play havoc with games, particularly with rugger, for which thirty players are required if a house is to field both a first and a second team. And there are elaborate strategies and timings which may be upset among that ambitious *élite* for which (in our particular nomenclature) house caps are seen as a stepping-stone to school colours. Here again it is the older boys who are most in the picture and the under-fifteens whom nobody much bothers about. Once the threat is established there are everywhere to be observed beefy six-footers studying games lists from beneath furrowed brows with much the concentration of alarmed citizens confronting ominous chalkings-up during the plague in Shakespeare's London.

# V

THE NEXT EPISODE I have to chronicle is the visit, some weeks later, of Robin Hayes's uncle, Jasper Tandem. He had made an appointment with me and arrived on the dot— which was a proper preliminary to seeking out a nephew under my care. It was indeed my first impression that he was proper all over: a well-groomed middle-aged man, dressed and comporting himself in a manner that stopped just short of formality, without any premature expression of anxiety lest he should be encroaching unjustifiably upon my time, but also without evincing any disagreeable disposition to settle in. I think I had prepared myself to receive one whose achieving of a near-corner in the peddling of canned popular music (not to speak of 'sleazy clip-joints') would be reflected in a considerable confidence, or even loudness, of address. But Mr Tandem was not at all like that. If there was anything of excess about him, it seemed to lie in the direction of the unassuming or even the diffident. It struck me that in this he was exceedingly unlike his sister, Mrs Hayes, either as I recalled her, or as her son had described her to me, or as the letter I had received from her exhibited. I speculated as to whether the misfortune which had befallen Mr Hayes had somehow impaired the confidence of his brother-in-law. I even wondered—although it seemed an unworthy idea—whether this so correct Jasper Tandem had himself fallen a little short of financial probity in his own professional affairs, and was as a consequence disturbed by the spectacle currently on view at Hutton Green. And it was of Hutton Green that Mr Tandem almost at once began to speak.

'If I have come in the first place to see my nephew,' he said, 'and to buck him up as well as I can if he seems in need of it, I have also had it in mind to thank you most sincerely for your great kindness in visiting my poor brother-in-law in his prison. My sister, too, is most grateful, and has charged me to assure you of the fact.'

'I could scarcely do less, Mr Tandem, Robin being a Heynoe boy.'

'She also bids me tell you how touched she was that you took the trouble to write to her so kindly afterwards.'

This was a bit steep. I had indeed managed a brief note to Mrs Hayes, since decency had demanded it. But that the woman had really sent me these messages I somehow didn't believe for a moment. Tandem had merely judged that a fiction of this sort would be agreeable to me.

'What I discussed with your brother-in-law,' I said, 'was the question of Robin's future career. And I suppose the problem does a little fall within my province. But our talk was really very brief, although the prison people set no limit to our interview. I gathered that Mr Hayes doesn't favour the idea of Robin being called to the bar.'

'It would cost money.' Tandem said this in a sensibly matter-of-fact fashion. 'What do you think yourself, Mr Syson? Or rather, what do you think of the boy in a general way? How would you describe his character?'

Although there was nothing challenging in the way these questions were delivered, I was a little put to a stand by them. When parents catechized me in similar terms I commonly did my best to manage a faithful reply, perhaps tempered at need in the interest of tact or charity. But parents are one thing, and uncles and aunts are quite another. I felt—and with an almost disconcerting force—that my visitor had no right to demand from me, in this stand-and-deliver fashion, an account of the light in which I regarded his nephew.

But this was an intemperate reaction. The man had as much title to be concerned for Robin as I had, and it would be injudicious to produce only some sort of snubbing response. Tandem, I recalled, might be proposing to invest hard cash in Robin Hayes, and as a business man he would feel it only prudent to vet his prospect in advance. If I happened to have concluded, on the strength of what was necessarily a certain amount of close

59

observation, that there was something flighty or unreliable in Robin's character, there would almost be an obligation upon me to speak about the boy at least with some reserve. As I had concluded nothing of the sort, I must not, through any appearance of hesitation, convey what would be a false impression.

'Robin is an excellent lad,' I said. 'His temperament is generous, and if he is sometimes impulsive it is in a thoroughly wholesome way. And there's what I'd call a useful hardness somewhere in his constitution. When he has made up his mind to a thing, he'll go straight ahead and put it through. He is far from afraid to come to judgement, even on difficult and painful matters. And when his feelings are clear to him, he commands considerable pungency in expressing them.'

I surprised myself not a little in the course of this speech. It wasn't the kind of thing I was accustomed to writing in end-of-term reports. Tandem contrived to receive my remarks as if a profound wisdom inhered in them. Then he asked a further question.

'Would you say he has many friends—or is he the sort that goes in for just one particular crony?'

'I think Robin's chief friend—naturally, perhaps—is his fellow house-prefect. A very steady boy called Macleod. I'm not sure how many other boys he's particularly friendly with.'

'I seem to remember, Mr Syson, that when one has attained to being one of the top boys of a school—in the sixth, and a prefect, and all the rest of it—one can feel a little short of anybody to admire any longer. Would that be at all Robin's position, do you think?' Tandem glanced at me sharply. 'And with any particular boy?'

'I can only say that I haven't thought at all on the question—whether in regard to Robin's position or to that of anybody else. For that matter, I doubt whether what you say about the issue in general has much truth to it.' I had begun to feel something uncomfortable in the drift of this conversation. 'No doubt anything like hero-worship is ruled out among senior boys. But they have come to know a good many of their contemporaries thoroughly well, and to distinguish in them qualities they are generous enough to admire as they should. Robin, for example, is admired because he has exceptionally safe hands with a rugger ball.'

Mr Tandem received this rather stuffy speech (as I suppose it was) with a bow that appeared to acknowledge the receipt of a further hand-out of wisdom. But he wasn't yet finished with the train of thought he had embarked on.

'Of course I also remember, Mr Syson, how in one's last year or couple of years one has the satisfaction of helping younger boys—at least in one's own house—to find their feet, and so on. It's a protective instinct coming into play, and a good and elevating thing.' This time, Robin's uncle plainly felt that he was getting going with wisdom himself—if in his always decorous way. 'And sometimes it can be a matter of just one younger boy, so that there is a certain element of romance to it. Or am I wrong?'

Wrong or right, the man had a bee in his bonnet—and it was a bee whose buzz I had heard before, particularly at the mildly penitential dinners of those Old Boy associations which it is incumbent upon a schoolmaster to attend from time to time. Just as there are some men who, according to the psychologists, have never succeeded in breaking free from the womb, so are there others who have similarly failed to leave school; who go on living a schoolboy's fantasies in a hung-up way, and whose curiosities can embarrassingly reveal themselves as distinctly immature. This pop-music man was one of them.

To those who, like myself, have chosen to work in schools as a means of earning their bread, there is something tiresome in the spectacle of grown men frequenting such institutions in a purely nostalgic way. There is, moreover, what may be called a small sub-species of such persons whose interest in adolescent life is of a predatory character, and of these it is irresponsible not to beware. But I had no reason to believe that my present visitor belonged here—or at least no reason sufficiently pronounced to warrant my showing any wish to be rid of him. And Mr Tandem was now on his feet, as if our interview were concluded to his satisfaction. It turned out, however, that he had something further to say, and that the occasion for this might have been very like a telepathic perception of what had been going on in my own head.

'I hope you don't mind my having come down,' he said. 'It has always been rather a habit of mine: inquiring, you know, into a situation on the spot.' Mr Tandem paused as if this merited an approbatory word. I failed to manage anything of the sort, not having much cared for 'situation'. The word seems to suggest that some sort of cleaning-up process may be required. And I didn't think that Heynoe called for anything of the kind.

'What small success I've had,' Tandem went on, 'has depended a good deal on that. I speak of business, of course. The discos and the youth clubs—particularly the religious ones, which are much more important than has been realized. And, of course, all those big festivals in parks and places. And the love-in affairs: there's a lot doing at them. So I keep on dropping in. Informing myself. And taking action as required.'

'Most interesting,' I said. 'And now I'll find a boy to hunt out Robin for you.' This was my common formula with visiting relations.

'Ah, yes—Robin, Mr Syson. I assure you he is constantly in my mind. His situation being as it is, you will understand that I feel myself to be entirely *in loco parentis* to him.'

'No doubt, Mr Tandem.' I reflected that this phrase had been very much in my own head. 'Of course we must remember that Robin has legally come of age. Whether young men still hold twenty-firsters at the university, I don't know. But men most of them are while still in their final year at school. The change since our own day is a mere legalism for the most part. But I've known it turn out something more than that.'

I was moving over to the door of my study as I offered these remarks, which were prompted by the feeling that I had been rather less than forthcoming in a conversable way. But Mr Tandem raised a restraining hand.

'Please don't disturb yourself,' he said. 'I'm in no need of a guide.' He glanced at his watch. 'And I know just where Robin is to be found. At your admirable swimming-pool, is it not? We must be glad that he is making the effort to overcome that odd disability of his. I approve of his resolution. And I've no doubt you do, too.'

I doubt whether I managed a reply. In this quite short interview I had moved from the impression that Jasper Tandem was at least less 'wicked' than his nephew had painted him to the persuasion that the more one saw of him the less pleasing was he likely to prove. There was no reason why he shouldn't know about Robin's current habits. The boy presumably wrote a weekly letter home, and such routine letters tend to be filled out with an enumeration of routine activities. Mrs Hayes must have learnt about the swimming sessions, and have passed the information on to her brother when hearing that he proposed to visit the school. Yet I didn't like the man's so brusquely asserting that he knew his way around, and I had the habit of regarding some sort of escort about the place to be the polite thing to summon up when visitors appeared. But I didn't really much bother about this on the present occasion. Tandem had the air of a man who has fixed himself up with something thoroughly agreeable, and when he took himself off I turned at once to other matters.

He was back within an hour, apparently from some sense of punctilio. I had to be shaken hands with in a valedictory manner.

'I've seen Robin,' he said. 'But he wasn't swimming. He was playing rugger. I had a chat with him in the changing-room afterwards, and then we strolled round the place. Very pleasant. And how it comes back to one: that smell of steamy boys and steamy towels.'

'Ah, yes.' I saw no need much to respond to this. 'If he's back on the football-field, that will be something satisfactory to the House. They've been missing him there.'

'The swimming was very much half-cock.' Tandem reported this with some appearance of momentary displeasure. 'I had a word or two with the fellow Vass. None too civil. I just mention the fact.' The silence with which I naturally received this didn't seem to disconcert my visitor. 'But you'll be glad to know that I think things are now likely to go quite well. There's been a certain amount of strain, of course. I hope to have relieved it to some extent.' Perhaps to give me confidence in this cheerful view of things, Mr Tandem produced a momentary and elusive smile. 'In fact, I think you will find the boy relaxed. It's the word, decidedly it's the word, that occurs to me. But if problems do arise, my dear Mr Syson, please get in touch with me at once.'

I didn't know quite how to respond to this request, since I had received no word from either of the Hayes parents that Jasper Tandem was to be treated as, so to speak, an ambassador or deputy head of family. But I reminded myself again that there might be money for Robin in this tiresome uncle, and that on humouring the man might depend getting the boy to Oxford and subsequently into a career. So I made some non-committal reply—whereupon Tandem proved to have a further request to bring forward.

'I'm putting up for the night at the Three Feathers,' he said. 'It's not at all a bad pub of its kind. So would you be agreeable to my having young Robin out to dinner? I let him know I'd ask you.'

'But of course.' It was something in the man's favour that he should request this leave on his nephew's part rather than simply announce an intention. 'Are you thinking of having him with a friend?'

'Well, no—although it's perhaps the usual thing. Without making heavy weather of it, my dear Syson, I feel I ought to get a little further with the boy in the way of discussing family affairs.'

'Very naturally.' I wasn't disposed to quarrel with Tandem over 'my dear Syson', although I thought it not wholly appropriate to a first meeting.

'I said I'd expect him at half past seven. I hope that doesn't conflict with any of his duties here in the House?'

'Not in the least.' I was a little impatient with this massive parade of correctness. 'Quite as a matter of course, his friend Macleod will take over anything of the kind.'

'Then that's capital. At what time has he to be back?'

'It's entirely up to him. He has a key.'

'Dear me! *Tempora mutantur, nos et mutamur in illis*—eh, Syson?' Quite unreasonably, no doubt, I judged this canned-music person to be turning intolerable again—chucking at me thus what he probably thought of as my own dusty stuff. But I had persevered with him, and must continue to do so for a further couple of minutes. So I said what came into my head.

'It's the Head of House's job,' I explained, 'to let in, and lock up behind, any senior boy who has permission to stay out up to eleven o'clock. If that's exceeded, the janitor's job passes to me.'

'And there's prompt discipline, eh?'

'Discipline, certainly, but not of the kind you are perhaps supposing, Mr Tandem. In Heynoe we get along not too badly, on the whole, while managing to behave in a tolerably civilised way.'

Tandem received this snub (for it was that) with a slight old-world bow. He was disappointed in me. So at last we parted, with mutual civilities. Quite obscurely, I was left with the feeling that there was something about the man, and about his visit, that I hadn't got to the bottom of. I reflected that he belonged to a world totally unknown to me.

Had Robin not thus been booked for the evening, I'd have sent for him and had a chat. But as things stood I sent for Iain Macleod instead. It wasn't quite the proper course, since in a way it represented going behind Robin's back. But I remembered how concerned Macleod had been that over his friend's troubles he and I should enter at need into a confidential relationship. And it seemed to me, although I couldn't quite have formulated a reason why, that some such need was heaving up over the horizon. It may have been Tandem's use of that word 'relaxed' that alerted me. I didn't believe in it for a moment. It had been in effect a lie which Robin's uncle had indulged in for his own amusement. And there was something almost sinister about this. I had to walk warily.

'So you've got back your wing three-quarter,' I said. I had decided against taking a devious route into our discussion. 'What's his form like, after all that splashing around in Vass's puddle?'

'Tiptop.' Macleod paused on this. He might have been himself a near-beginner in Vass's puddle, uncertain of what would happen if he ventured head-first into it. 'Robin's playing like a demon.' he said.

'That sounds excellent.'

'But it isn't. I can't tell you quite why, sir, but it isn't. It's almost as you shouldn't play in practice—or ever.'

'Good heavens—you can't mean he's giving people a rough time? Three-quarters can't do that, even if they feel like it. They've got hands and legs, not feet.'

'Yes, of course.' Although deadly serious, Macleod contrived a fleeting polite acknowledgement that I had spoken in an informed and succinct manner. "It's that horrible business about his father, I suppose. Or that chiefly.' Macleod frowned. 'Getting him down. Or up, really—into a kind of active desperation. He brings it on field along with his boots and gumshield.'

'Did you meet his uncle this afternoon?'

'Yes—it was rather odd. This Mr Tandem came barging in—pretty well dodging through the showers, you might say—after practice. We were quite surprised.'

'It was nostalgia, Iain. He liked the smell. He told me so.' I had been unable to resist this absurdity. 'You were led out dripping and introduced to him?'

'Well, yes—in a way. I don't think Robin at all expected him. Then he carried Robin off for what he called a pow-wow. I saw Robin only for a few minutes afterwards, and there was something funny about him. I don't *mean* funny. Strange.'

'That sounds rather worrying.' I felt that either Macleod was getting out of his depth or that I was perhaps forcing him into a false position. There might, in fact, be something in his friend's situation that he didn't, after all, feel entitled to tell me about. So I asked what seemed at least a harmless question. 'Why should you think Robin was surprised at his uncle's turning up? Robin mentioned it to me some time ago as likely to happen.'

'I see. Well, what I was thinking about was Robin's once having told me that his uncle hated places like this because of his having been superannuated.'

'Superannuated, Iain?'

'It's what they call—or used to call—being expelled.'

'So it was, at some schools.'

'Uncle Jasper had been sacked, and it had put him against public schools in a permanent way. I asked Robin if he knew *why* he'd been sacked. He said it had probably been because of the usual thing. In those days, you know, they pretty well had your balls off for it—or at least hanged you by the neck until you were dead. The reckless Jasper hadn't been content with the quiet pleasures of D.I.Y.'

I need hardly say that I found this speech from the staid Iain Macleod astonishing. I always encouraged freedom of utterance around me. Short of a mere senseless use of four-letter words (which they'd scarcely employ anyway) I liked to hear from my boys whatever they'd hear from one another. But this—although not without a stroke of wit—had been a little extreme. And what I seemed to hear in it was the voice less of Iain Macleod than of Robin Hayes: of that new and harder Robin Hayes who had been brought into being by the state of affairs climaxing in Hutton Green.

'Robin seems to have got some way with his swimming,' I said, by way of changing the subject. 'But then he seems to have felt that a man can learn to swim at any time, but that the days are numbered in which he can play rugger for his school or his house.'

'Well, yes.' Macleod hesitated for a moment. 'But there was a bit of a hitch as well.'

'So there was.'

'Robin told you about it?'

'Not Robin, as a matter of fact. Vass. He thought he ought to, since there had been some danger involved.'

'Yes—but it wasn't, you know, that Robin felt he'd made a fool of himself and was ashamed of showing himself in the pool again. He says he thinks hardly anybody noticed it. Except, of course, the brat who rescued him.' Again Macleod hesitated, and I saw with surprise that he had become agitated. 'Sir,' he said, 'I have complete confidence in you.'

Something like these words one may occasionally utter to an over-diffident boy. To hear them the other way on was distinctly odd.

'If you have something you want to tell me,' I said, 'and if you feel you ought to tell me, go ahead. Only take a moment to think.'

'I've taken a good many. And it's very simple, really. Or it *begins* by being very simple. Robin has become very fond of a boy in another house.'

'I see.' I wasn't, of course, particularly surprised by this information, since such attachments belong with the commonplaces of adolescence in schools like Helmingham. But I was astounded and, I suppose, alarmed by the way in which the information was coming to me. Iain Macleod was a boy who subscribed on the whole—or so I believed—to the general ethos of schools like Helmingham. He was also very intelligent; quite as intelligent as Robin Hayes. That he should come running to me bearing a tale (for so the thing could reasonably be represented) was a phenomenon for which a good deal of explanation was required.

'A younger boy?' I asked.

'Yes, of course. A second-year brat in School House called Daviot. David Daviot. A regular bit of crumpet, it seems. And of course as inaccessible as if he was in a nunnery.'

'Except when swimming.' I don't doubt I said this harshly, for 'crumpet' had upset me—its use in the present context appearing to me to vulgarize something not necessarily bad.

'Yes. Robin could at least go and gape. He'd come back to Helmingham pretty well to do that. So far, it's just pathetic. Like some rubbish out of Courtly Love.' Macleod paused on this learned allusion. 'But then, for School House brats, the swimming sessions suddenly packed up. The bug was raging among them, and every bratlet lodged blubbering in his chaste and lonely cot. Which is why Robin returned to the rugger field.'

For a moment I found nothing to say. Macleod seemed to share with his fellow-prefect a liability to be carried away by linguistic exuberance at the crisis of a narrative.

'And blubbering is the key to the thing,' Macleod went on. 'The brats have lost their nerve—and stiff little upper lip and so forth—and have told all.'

68

'All what, Iain?'

'All about School House. Of course everybody has known about it for quite some time. Or everybody except masters. Particularly Mr Taplow. He's our top stinks man is Taplow, no doubt. But there are stinks he wouldn't be aware of even if you stuck his head in them. And now the letters have been scrawled in the sick-beds and sent home. In no time the mothers will be queueing up in that second family car, and the fathers will be sitting down to write letters to *The Times*. So there's the background to Robin's present state of mind. School House is in the middle of a reign of terror or worse. Ever since last term. And this David is in the thick of it.'

'About School House, Iain, I've been listening to nonsense of one kind or another for getting on for thirty years. Are you sure this isn't just more of it? I don't mean about Robin's fondness for a junior boy there, which I won't hastily censure, but that there has been some large outbreak of bullying throughout the house. Is that what you're saying?'

'Oh, yes—that, certainly.'

'And a collapse of morale in other ways as well?'

'You name it, they have it.'

'Iain, stop talking in that fashion. It's a kind of funk in face of something it's no doubt unpleasant for you to feel you have to talk about at all. And I still find it hard to believe—particularly of School House, which seems to go in for quiet and studious boys.'

'Sorry, sir. I know it's not a thing for perky chat. But it's a terrific facer for Robin, and I'm upset about it. But it's true that it sometimes happens, isn't it? Really just another kind of bug.'

'Well, yes. Winchester had a famous reign of terror for some weeks about a hundred years ago. Letters in *The Times*, all right, and the Head Master and his senior assistants professing themselves ignorant and astounded. And no doubt in varying degree in plenty of other schools since then. As for Helmingham, it's true we've had our tough phases from time to time. But nothing to any point of outright scandal. And don't think, Iain, that I suppose you to be making a mountain out of a molehill. You're too sensible for that. So it's upsetting. As for Robin, we must do what we can.'

'There's another funny thing, although I don't suppose it's important. This little Daviot is the son of the judge who put Robin's father in gaol.'

'The grandson, actually.' I was glad to show myself as well-informed at least on this minor aspect of the matter. 'But the boy's parents are dead, and his grandfather is his guardian.'

'I see. Was he particularly hard on Mr Hayes—in sentencing him, I mean?'

'Rather the opposite, if anything. But I've heard he's a very severe man with professional criminals.' I fell silent for some moments on this, feeling there was nothing to be gained by thus passing on to irrelevant matters. 'Robin is going out to dinner with his uncle this evening, Iain. I'll think over what we've been discussing—and take no action before I've had another word with you. What you've told me is no more than advance notice of what would come to me anyway in time, and I wouldn't like Robin to get the notion you'd been telling secrets.'

'Of course I'm going to tell Robin I've been doing just that. I shan't enjoy it. But it will be the proper thing.'

'So it will,' I said.

The rest of that evening was variously irritating. Several boys banged on my door in order to make trivial and vexatious requests or demands of one sort or another. The muted sounds of what seemed to be more tramping and shouting than usual assailed me through the green baize doors which were supposed to insulate me from the legitimate *brio* of healthy juvenile life. But what really disturbed me was the new light I had received on my Head of House.

It must not be thought that I was particularly alarmed by the mere fact of Robin's having formed a romantic attachment to a younger boy. It was rather the association established in my mind between this fact and something insidiously disagreeable in the conversation of Robin's uncle that obscurely irked me. Or this taken along with something else. It was now necessary to believe that Robin hadn't in the least wanted to come back to Helmingham in order to help me to run Heynoe as it should be run. Anything of the kind that he had intimated to the dons, and also through the Head Master during my absence in Vermont, had been largely disingenuous. With his father's disgrace as no more than a concomitant factor, he had wanted on that side of things only what he had eventually confessed to as respectable seniority and a private life. His real object had been as much as he could contrive of the sight and society of this small boy, Daviot—the impulse being much strengthened, no doubt, by a laudable wish to protect Daviot from an unwholesome state of affairs already believed to be building up in School House. That Daviot was the grandson of a particular circuit or High Court judge was a slightly bizarre but not essentially relevant aspect of the situation.

I took a second look at this last thought and saw that it wasn't strictly true; was not, indeed, fair to Robin. That it had been to Mr Justice Daviot that there had fallen the duty of clapping Mr Hayes into gaol must have been thoroughly upsetting in itself, and I ought to remember this when inclined to feel that my top boy had been less than candid with me.

It was my custom at that time to preside over and share the boys' midday meal, and to have my housekeeper provide a civilized supper to which I sometimes invited a guest or guests, but more commonly ate alone. I was on my own on this particular evening, and I had just finished my glass of wine and settled down with a book when I was called to the telephone.

'Tim here,' Tim Taplow's voice said. 'Do I disturb you at piquet with Miss Sparrow?'

'Nothing of the kind.' This was a joke of Taplow's of which I had grown rather tired. But I made my reply with good humour, since it occurred to me that perhaps he had become belatedly aware that all was not well in his house, and was anxious to have the benefit of such experience as I possessed. 'I believe the lady's at the Staffords', as a matter of fact, playing bridge.'

'Then can I hop over, Robert, and consult you about that grand old fortifying classical curriculum?' This was another established joke. 'It's this boy of mine, Dunlop, you know. He's determined to storm Corpus and win all those prizes for Greek verse and what have you. You know far more about his chances than I do. So . . .'

'Of course I do, Tim, It wouldn't be all that difficult, would it? Yes, do come over straight away. Port or brandy?'

'The first first and then the second. And beer as a chaser later on.'

There had been something forced about this jocular injunction, and I wasn't sure that Taplow really had nothing but the ambitious Dunlop in his head. So I made the necessary hospitable arrangements and prepared to be enlightened on the point. It turned out that the Corpus postulant was a genuine anxiety of his housemaster's, as he already was of mine. We spent the better part of an hour in sorting him out, during which time Taplow made little progress with his glass of port. But he then sat back and abruptly asked a question.

'Robert, whatever made you accept a house? You hadn't kids to educate, or even a wife to take to Margate or to gay Paree. And I've been told you were the sort of chap who can keep up his scholarship even while teaching school. Explain.'

'It's simple enough, Tim.' The implication that I was no longer 'that sort of chap' didn't offend me. Candour is a prime possession of schoolboys, and a sense of its value at all times perhaps a little rubs off on their teachers. 'I've always liked young people, whether boys or girls. I sometimes think that if Helmingham went co-educational—and quite soon we're going to see a number of such schools taking the plunge—I'd be one of those who wouldn't turn a hair, even although it was happening more or less at the end of my time. I like to see more of my pupils' minds than the chunks they pass examinations with. I think that's your answer.'

'Co-education—and co-residence, which is the nub—certainly deserve thinking about.' This time, Taplow did address himself adequately to his glass. 'Is there essentially something brutalizing—not that that's not too strong a word—about sexual segregation in adolescence? It's a question we must all ask ourselves at times. Only I can't say I've ever been pertinacious about it myself. I tend, you know, to shy away from conundrums to which scientific method can't really be applied.'

Taplow now drained his port with a very improper gulp. 'Hell!' he said. 'What I'm skating round is the fact that some sort of lid has blown off School House. The bug has done it. For quite some time there have been goings-on that neither Jane nor I managed to tumble to.' Jane was Taplow's wife.

'How is the bug?' I asked—I suppose by way of gaining time in face of this sudden unveiling of anxiety. 'More or less over?'

'Yes, I hope so. The juniors are out of quarantine and around again.'

'I'm delighted to hear it.'

'But it got them down and they came out with tales of woe. For some stupid reason School House has always been a bit of a butt. And now we're going to have to face more than a whiff of scandal. You must have heard all about it already.'

'Only a vague word.'

'Vague words are the worst. There have certainly been some high jinks, as well as pretty low ones, I ought to have had my eye on. I'm thinking of asking young Johncock to move in on us. The school makes him pay for his flat, you know, so he'd gain some advantage from the arrangement. And he might get around and make the young beasts toe the line a bit. It's just an idea. And there's quite a lot to be said for Johncock. On the side of mere mystique, he has no use for places like Helmingham.'

Although far from certain that this was a recommendation in itself, I refrained from expressing any doubt about Johncock. It definitely looked as if Taplow required a companion on the bridge. And Johncock, so markedly a no-nonsense character, might serve in the office very well. But one point did occur to me.

'Of course, Tim, you have to think ahead. These troubles suddenly start up in a house—and then as suddenly blow over. And when that happened you might find yourself landed with the man until he went to another school.'

'I've enough to do, thinking of the present week. Two letters from mums this morning, Robert. And in no time a dad or two may be weighing in. And nowadays so many of them just don't know the drill! They're capable of writing straight to the Head Man about Billy or Bobby having his arm twisted.'

'Certainly they are.' It seemed to me that the deterioration in the morale of School House had extended itself to the housemaster's study. And I was curious to know whether one problematical situation had come to its occupant's awareness. 'Dads are bad,' I said. 'But uncles are worse. I had a call from a pestilent one this afternoon. My top boy at the moment is his nephew. A capable lad called Robin Hayes. I don't know whether you've come across him?'

'I think not. I don't recall the name. One of your out-and-out humanists, I expect. So I won't have taught him.'

'Probably not. The man's excuse for coming to see me was that the boy's father has had the misfortune to be put in gaol. But you won't have heard of that.'

'Definitely not, Robert. My life's too crowded to be studying the Newgate Calendar. And I'd imagine that in any one term several Helmingham boys have a father doing time.'

'I think that may be an exaggeration. But what I was going to say was that there's an odd link-up between my boy's father and the grandfather of one of yours. An old gentleman called Daviot.'

'Ah, yes. He came to see me when his grandson was enrolled. A formidable old person. Some sort of judge.'

'Yes—and it was he who sent the father of my boy Hayes to prison. Incidentally, the boys were at the same prepper.' I paused for a moment, and got no reaction to this. It had become evident that the situation of David Daviot, so intolerable in the regard of Robin Hayes, was not in the mind of Tim Taplow as a significant part of his current problem. And about that problem I had now been sympathetic enough. So I led the talk to other things. We had got very comfortably to the brandy—although not to the beer—when my guest at length glanced at his watch.

'Good lord!' he said. 'After eleven o'clock. I must be on my way, Robert. Heynoe's a great comfort, you know. Just purrs along: good order and good feeling and a blessed quiet everywhere.' This was perhaps a slightly barbed speech, and Taplow—who had cheered up a little during the preceding half-hour—glanced at me almost mischievously as he got to his feet.

Then, as if at a signal given, from just outside my study came

74

the sound of a door violently thrown open, followed by that of much shattered and falling glass.

I should explain that when boys returned to Heynoe late at night it was by way of the front door to my own part of the House and not by their normal daytime entrance. It was a door directly opposite my study, across a fairly spacious hall, and it thus came about that within a couple of seconds of this unholy din—and with Taplow close behind me—I was surveying the disgraceful cause of it. I was surveying Robin Hayes, that is to say, now standing in the middle of the hall, and swaying uncommonly oddly on his feet. In fact he was very drunk, and behind him was the shocking spectacle of my front door decidedly in disrepair. Having become aware of unsatisfactory behaviour on the part of his latch-key, Robin had used a vigorous kick to further his entrance. And unfortunately my own golf-clubs, thrust within their bag at an awkward angle in an umbrella stand, had produced a surprising shambles far and wide in the hall. There was even blood involved, some flying splinter of glass having gashed one of Robin's hands. And the boy was contriving to glare wildly around him, much as if he had been precipitated into a bandits' den.

Nor were Tim Taplow and I the only observers of this irregular state of affairs. Iain Macleod had appeared through the door giving on the boys' side of the house, and I realized that he must have been on an anxious look-out for his friend's belated return from his dinner engagement. I realized, too, that Macleod had as yet no notion of the actual situation confronting him; that he was imagining a street accident or something of the sort. When he spoke, it was to confirm this.

'Robin,' he said, 'are you all right? Are there others?' But as he asked these questions, light broke on him. 'Jesus,' he said, 'Jesus *Christ!*' The ejaculation didn't sound profane. It might have come from a wholly pious boy—which Iain Macleod almost certainly was not. As he uttered it, he put out a hand and laid it on Robin's arm protectively or warningly—something it came to me that I had never seen one boy do to another before. 'You're ill,' he said. 'Bad oysters or something. Come to bed.'

75

And Taplow and I were not the sole observers of this scene. Into the light of an exterior lamp over the front door had walked John Stafford and Miss Sparrow. They were already mounting the steps when I first became aware of them, and the spectacle bewildered me until I recalled the bridge party. It hadn't broken up until late and the Head Master, with his habitual routine courtesy, had escorted the lady back to Heynoe.

These two were now in the hall, and surveying the scene. It would have been my matron's impulse, thus suddenly confronted with a contretemps not within her sphere, to murmur a couple of words and mount to her own flat. But this Miss Sparrow did not do. Her eye had been on the Head Master, and she had spotted the fact that he was moved to take charge of the situation. It would have been a false step, for if Helmingham was his school Heynoe was my house. Miss Sparrow took a step of her own, a single forward step, and held out a hand.

'Thank you so much, Head Master,' she said, 'for seeing me safely home. Good night.'

Stafford took the offered hand, and departed like a lamb. I imagine he was grateful to the woman for saving him from an unsuitable move. He wouldn't, of course, refrain from expressing interest in the episode later on. But that was unimportant. I had a new problem to think about.

'Robin,' I said, 'Iain is right. You'd better be off to bed. And don't make a row. It's getting on for midnight.'

Perhaps I ought to have known that it would be unwise to lay even the ghost of an injunction on the boy in his present condition. Certainly the result of having done so was unfortunate. So far, Robin had shown no awareness of anybody's presence except Macleod's. But now he looked at me; appeared to get me, if uncertainly, into focus; took several stumbling steps in my direction. I saw that he was carrying a slip of paper in his uninjured hand. With this he suddenly lunged forward, and just failed to flip me in the face.

'Robin, you bloody fool!' This came from Macleod in a shout, and it was evident that his distress had turned for the moment into fury. He made a grab at his friend; there was a scuffle; but the grab proved to be an expert one. Robin was whirled helplessly round, with an arm twisted between his shoulder-blades. Then, as sometimes happens to quite a small boy, he was propelled forward with a knee in his bottom, and disappeared through that green baize door.

I ought to have been outraged by all this indignity beneath my nose. But, in fact, I was rather in a state of shock. Drunken young men can be variously intolerable, but it is not (I believe) a condition in which they are likely to act wholly out of character. And that insolent gesture of Robin's towards me had surely to be so described. Certainly it had bewildered and acutely pained me—much as if a son of my own had performed an insulting act.

'And so to bed,' Tim Taplow said. 'For us, too. Even in Heynoe, Robert, one can have something to think about.' He took a quick glance at me, and I saw him flush. 'I beg your pardon,' he said. 'Miss Sparrow, good night.' And Taplow bolted through what remained of my battered front door.

So Matron and I were left alone on our territory, and after a short silence I asked an almost inconsequent question.

'That scrap of paper the boy had.' I said. 'What was it?'

'I think,' Miss Sparrow said, 'it was a cheque. And now I must see if poor Robin will let me bandage that hand.'

And the admiral's daughter, who was seldom without an immediate duty, herself departed to the boys' side of the House.

# VI

THESE EVENTS TOOK place on a Saturday, and I need hardly say that I woke up on the Sunday morning wondering what I ought to do about them. The wise answer seemed to be, 'Not too much'. If an eighteen-year-old youth feels for one reason or another pretty miserable, and if he goes out to dine with an intemperate older companion and ends up much the worse for drink, it is his own affair and should be so regarded. If at an Oxford or Cambridge college such a young man demonstrates his condition by breaking a few windows he will have to pay for the repair of them; if his behaviour has been yet more objectionable he will have to present himself before some dean or censor, submit to brisk admonishment, and at least suffer a fine to be chalked up against him in the college books. But unless some extreme grossness has been involved, there the matter will end.

I could see that in a boarding-school, even though the youth be of almost the same age, different conditions must be taken into account. Oxford and Cambridge colleges get along without prefects, so on nobody is imposed the duty of setting an example to anybody else. And there are no younger boys around, to be startled and perhaps frightened by the spectacle of inebriety in one of whom they are expected to be to a certain extent in awe. There was a further trickiness in Robin Hayes's position in this regard. As Head of House he was accountable to me, and in practice to me alone. But the office made him, *ipso facto*, a school prefect as well. In other words, the previous night's occurrence was John Stafford's problem as much as it was mine.

That the Head Master (not to speak of Miss Sparrow) had, as it may be expressed, walked in on the act struck me as not altogether unfortunate. I'd have had to tell Stafford about the incident anyway. Now the natural thing would be that he would take the initiative in contacting me with some temperately phrased inquiry as to what I felt about the background of the affair. But what *did* I feel? Whatever Stafford concluded, it was at least clear to me that I must without loss of time have it out with Robin personally. But I'd give myself—by way of ordering matters in my own head—until after School Prayers that morning.

Helmingham was from its inception a strongly Anglican school. As in many similar schools, the chapel dominates the scene. It is a huge affair, with a capacity which must have been vastly in excess of its first complement of boys: a formidable expression of the ethos governing nineteenth-century upper middle-class education. A lofty structure in Butterfield's best Gothic manner, it has niched over its west portal an uncommonly good copy (it might almost be a replica) of Donatello's St George as carved for Or San Michele. This, a later embellishment, must have been the gift of a wealthy Old Boy of cultivated taste. Martial saints and knights are also prominent in the stained glass. In the great west window is St George again, this time grappling with his dragon—a writhing brute which the school variously allegorized as German Militarism, the Tobacco Industry, the Demon Drink, and Sex Rearing its Ugly Head. In lancets on each side of this, Sir Gareth and Sir Geraint set out on their respective quests—the first without his taunting but irresistible Lynette, and the second with the unfortunate Enid, drooping behind her leash of horses laden with an ironmonger's stock of armour, well out of the picture.

In this temple of muscular Christianity Helmingham boys formerly spent a good deal of time through every day of a twelve-week term, but by the period of which I write this regimen had been relaxed, and devotions were compulsory on Sunday mornings alone. It by no means followed that the chapel was unoccupied at other times. Every school has its minority of extremely religious boys, and Helmingham happened to possess in a certain Father Edwards an elderly chaplain who was popular not only with the pious but with the profane as well—this universality of appeal being contributed to by the fact Father Edwards owned a keen interest in theatrical concerns of a non-ecclesiastical sort, and was a moving spirit in the mounting and producing of school plays. But the religious boys kept him very busy in the chapel throughout the week. They insisted on a great deal of auricular confession, experimented with censers and asperges, and organized mini-services designed to convert their contemporaries in the surrounding villages.

But School Prayers on Sunday—a kind of matins—is the great occasion. On weekdays the boys wear, and have always worn, skimpy black-stuff gowns in class; at School Prayers they appear, as do the masters, in surplices. They like this, since all boys like dressing up, and the spectacle of these virginal rows of healthy youth particularly pleases those parents, of whom there are always a good many, who are week-ending in the neighbourhood for the purpose of entertaining their sons and their sons' friends. To this soothing institution I betook myself on the morrow of Robin Hayes's disastrous ill-conduct.

The boys sit house by house and in more or less prescriptive places: the small fry at the front and on a lower level than their seniors. We prayed and made responses with precision; we sang Bunyan's hymn; we listened to a short sermon from Father Edwards. Perhaps betrayed by an exceptional mildness in the November air, Father Edwards drifted from rugger to cricket when in search of metaphors, and we heard a good deal about the Great Scorer and what He is best pleased to have notched up at the end of the game. The boys listened to this familiar homily, straight out of the age of Sir Henry Newbolt, not so much with an appearance of polite interest as in a kind of friendly inattentiveness. The Head Master, who sat a little higher than anybody else, showed himself as exempt from listening at all, since he spent every minute of the service in gazing, or seeming to gaze, successively into the heart of each individual among the six hundred boys before him. This systematic exercise must have been alarming to new boys subjected to it. But the school as a whole accepted the scrutiny as part of the show, and there was always a feeling of disappointment when it happened that on one Sunday or another Stafford failed to turn up.

Towards the end of the sermon I found I was myself doing a certain amount of scrutinizing. It chanced that I sat in my stall (a station of some minor dignity) just opposite the boys of School House, and I was trying to decide which of them was that David Daviot for whose sake—I had to face it—Robin Hayes had returned to Helmingham.

Being at the start of his second year at the school, David was likely to be one of the ten or a dozen boys in the second pew from the front. He was probably—although Iain Macleod hadn't said so—good-looking. Yet this wasn't certain, since it might have been the pathos of an ugly duckling that had won Robin's heart. As he had lately been a captive of the bug, it was possible that David would still be looking a bit under the weather. Were it true that he had indeed been the object of bullying and even of sexual abuse, it was predictable that, if at all a sensitive plant, he would be very woebegone indeed.

What I saw was a row of perfectly healthy-looking small boys. Deprived of bottoms and equipped with wings, they might have served agreeably as a choir of cherubs in a sentimental late-Murillo type of picture. But to say this is, of course, to exaggerate their juvenility. They were probably without exception in their fifteenth year—but at a public school that counts as being a small boy still. Eighty or a hundred years before, they would all have been enduring rather a tough time, much as a matter of course. According alike to Macleod and to Tim Taplow's dawning sense of the situation, they were enduring just that now. I couldn't see that they showed any very obvious sign of this. Perhaps they had rapidly recuperated during their privileged quarantine while under illness or the threat of it. Boys do pick up quickly. . . . Suddenly I realized why these quite random thoughts were going through my head. I was dodging the consciousness that this pleasing row of boys, although cropped, tubbed, scrubbed and surpliced alike, were not uniform in every way. They were all, I suppose, reasonably personable lads. But one of them was very personable indeed. That he was David Daviot I didn't for a moment doubt. And my heart sank as I regarded him.

It would be no good going on to try to describe David—to say that he had blue eyes or golden curly hair (as he certainly had) or this sort of mouth or that sort of nose. I have very little sense of such appearances. I had no notion, for instance, whether this supremely pretty boy was or was not likely to mature into a handsome man. I just saw what had brought Robin Hayes in thrall. And I didn't like it a bit.

Tim Taplow was sitting almost opposite to me, looking worried and irritated. I imagine he was one of those conscientious unbelievers who are troubled at putting in even a formal appearance at any sort of religious service, but who hesitate to make what they would regard as self-important nuisances of themselves by consistently staying away. What occurred to me now was that on the previous evening I ought not to have avoided telling him everything I knew about his David Daviot and my Robin Hayes, and I resolved to do so as soon as the service was over. But he slipped off before I could get hold of him, and it was with Father Edwards that I found myself walking away from the chapel. What was running in my head bobbed up, all the same.

'Father,' I said—for Edwards liked to be addressed in this way— 'you know every soul in the place. Would the child at the end of the second row of School House go by the name of Daviot?'

'Yes, indeed, Robert. David Daviot. Puck.'

'Puck?' This perplexed me.

'Ah—I forgot you were in foreign parts last term. We did *A Midsummer-Night's Dream* as the summer play, and I gave Daviot the rôle of Puck. He had shown himself to be uncommonly precocious in the theatrical way. He got a lot of applause.' Father Edwards, although an old man encased within a heavy and trailing cassock, was striding vigorously forward. 'At the moment I'm worried about him, as a matter of fact.'

So was I. But I reflected that Edwards's worry was not necessarily the same as mine. Perhaps the boy was in his confirmation class, and—precocious in this field as well— expressing intellectual doubts which would make it difficult conscientiously to present him to the bishop when the appointed day came.

'Is he clever?' I asked tentatively.

'I don't know that he is. Certainly not *very* clever. Were he that, a small success wouldn't have turned his head.'

'I see.' In fact I judged this to be the generalization of one disposed to an optimistic view of human nature. 'Do you mean that his managing an attractive Puck has resulted in his becoming stage-struck?'

'Precisely that—or that and an incident he says took place in the holidays. I hardly know whether or not he be romancing.'

'What was the incident, Father?'

'Well, he says there must have been some sort of talent-scout present at our play. It's just possible. In fact, I've known it to occur. But that was when I happened to have the son of a distinguished actor in my cast. What Daviot says is that this man later approached him in a public park.'

'My dear Father!'

'Well, yes, Robert—yes. But Daviot was helping a younger cousin to sail a toy boat somewhere—perhaps in the Round Pond—when this person approached him and began talking about an audition with the B.B.C. The man said he hadn't gone to Daviot's home—which is, of course, in London—because he knew he had a very strict father—no, that's not right: grandfather—who wouldn't countenance any such distraction from the boy's studies. Those weren't David's words, but that was the gist of the thing.'

'And did the boy fall for it?'

'No, he didn't. He says that the man was "nosy"—asking him a lot about his particular friends at school, and that sort of thing.'

'Any boy is likely to resent that.'

'Yes, indeed. But I gathered young Daviot did chat to the fellow for quite some time, and then—quite why, I didn't gather—got uneasy at what he'd been induced to talk about, and the way things were going. So he says he said—and it's quite absurd—that he would have to consult his agent. And then he and his cousin struck sail, you may say, and went home. I suppose he had been frightened—and quite right, too.'

'It's an odd story, Father.'

'And completely made up? I thought so at the time. But

something equally odd has come under my observation since—here at school, and in the second week of term. I had gone down to our far meadow, which hardly anybody goes near, so it's a capital place for meditation. And there I had a glimpse of David Daviot talking to a strange man. Not, incidentally, a gentleman. I didn't interfere, but I mentioned the thing to Tim Taplow that evening. Tim didn't show much interest. I think he put me down as a senile old chap with a dirty mind.'

'In that case, Father, I'll own to a dirty mind too. The boy strikes me as a perfect *garçon fatal*—if such a thing may be.' I almost added, 'As a matter of fact, one of my senior lads in Heynoe is much taken up with him at this moment.' But I forbore. Edward was no doubt the man responsible for the spiritual welfare of the whole crowd of us. But he was not the first person to whom I should reveal—or was it betray?—the confidence which Iain Macleod had reposed in me. I hadn't even managed to speak to Taplow about it. And that, certainly, I ought by now to have done. This thought was becoming insistent with me.

So I took leave of our chaplain and went back to the House. I had barely got out of my surplice and thought of a drink when the telephone rang. I wasn't surprised.

'Syson, this is Stafford. Do I disturb you?'

'No, Head Master. You do not.'

'I thought that we ought to have a word—that I ought to seek a word of advice—about that small affair last night. I apologize for gate-crashing it. Was that Hayes? I had only a glimpse, you know.'

'Yes. Robin Hayes. My Head Boy.'

'Have you had a word with him since?'

'I haven't seen him since. And he wasn't in chapel.'

'He'll have to explain that, I suppose?'

'He will.'

'And the general circumstances of the thing as well?'

'Yes. I imagine, Head Master, that Hayes will do that when he comes to me to apologize, as I don't doubt he will do this afternoon.'

'Good, Syson. That sounds good. Of course there has been all this strain over his father. One sympathizes very much. Is it your impression that he just went out on a blind?'

'Definitely not. He was invited out to dinner by an uncle on his mother's side. A man called Jasper Tandem, who came to call on me beforehand. It was all perfectly regular.'

'Of course, of course. Was it a party for Hayes and some friends?'

'No. It was just the boy himself. His uncle said he wanted to talk family business with him. Something of that kind.'

'Then I'd suppose, Syson, that the fellow ought to have *noticed*. Don't you think? I mean that his nephew was drinking far too much. It strikes me as a little odd.'

'It strikes me, Head Master, as very odd indeed.' I suppose I was becoming annoyed by this thinly veiled interrogation. 'The thing has the appearance of having been downright malicious. I have formed an unfavourable impression of this Jasper Tandem.'

'That, Syson, of course weighs with me a great deal. Has the family situation resulted in this uncle's taking over responsibility for the boy in any formal way? Had you had anything of the kind communicated to you by the boy's mother or by a lawyer?'

'Nothing of the sort.'

'I suppose his returning his nephew to us dead drunk to be sufficient ground for my writing to him asking him not to visit Helmingham again. It's something I've had to do before—and if you advise it I'll do it in this case.'

'I'll bear it in mind, Head Master. Meanwhile, there's the question of Hayes's position in the school.'

'We go easy.' Stafford snapped this out with conviction. 'Demote your Head Boy while his father's in gaol, and you don't know where you are. Quite probably in the gutter press. And fortunately his lapse didn't happen exactly *coram publico*. That other lad was Macleod, wasn't he?'

'Yes.'

'A reliable boy. I know his people. And, of course, there was your Miss Sparrow, who bundled me out of the door pretty well before I'd taken in the state of play myself. You must find her an

85

invaluable woman, Syson.' Stafford paused for a moment. 'Capable of a quick decision when required.'

Whether I thought I deserved this one, I won't say. But I left it to Stafford to continue the talk if he found it useful to do so. And of course he did—to make a deft return to amenity.

'But, my dear Syson, it's entirely for you to decide. If you think the boy should be sent home, home he'll go.'

'To be sent home' was our school formula for expulsion. And it had been darkly in my mind that Stafford might have taken it into his head that Robin had better depart. So I was, in fact, relieved.

'I'll probably tell him,' I said, 'that he will be homeward bound if it happens again. That's only fair to him. But this time we'll lay all the blame on the bad uncle. Incidentally, I rather think he tipped the boy lavishly.' I am not sure why I went on to this unnecessary detail, except that Robin's action with what Miss Sparrow had said was a cheque was somehow coming to occupy a very uncomfortable position in my mind.

'Well, nothing could be more normal and blameless than that,' Stafford said—evidently slightly surprised. 'If I'd been visited by an uncle at Marlborough and hadn't made a quid out of it, I'd have been very aggrieved indeed. As you'd have been at poor old Harrow-on-the-Hill.'

A facetious remark of this sort was unlike John Stafford, and took me by surprise. I had been wondering whether I had a duty to tell him there and then that, as well as trouble at home, Robin Hayes had trouble of a different order in School House. But this I didn't now do, and our telephone conversation ended.

'About last night. I've come to apologize.'

As I had predicted, Robin was in my study that afternoon. He still looked physically disordered, and a slight down on his face suggested to me that he hadn't shaved. I ought to have been pleased that he had thus promptly turned up. But in fact I had felt that something was going to go wrong from the instant of his entering the room. Once or twice boys had been sent to me by a well-meaning colleague with a command to apologize to me about this or that. And they had done so with an icy formality which had been very disagreeable indeed. Nobody could have given Robin such an order on the present occasion (Miss Sparrow was far too sensible to have done so), but the effect was much as it had then been. Robin Hayes was in the presence of an enemy, or at least of somebody hopelessly in an enemy's camp.

'And to resign,' he said.

'Resign? Resign from what?'

'From being your Head Boy, of course. Unless it's unnecessary, because I'm going to be chucked out of the school. Iain tells me the Head Master was lurking around last night.'

'He certainly was not lurking. And you are certainly not going to be chucked out. That's his decision, just as it would be mine. As for resigning, Robin, I've heard that from you before. I've also heard you talk about the loyalty biznai. It's time you got going on it. I know that various difficulties and discouragements beset you—miseries, if you like. Nothing can be better for you in that situation than to grit your teeth and do your thing. And not take to the bottle. In fairness I have to mention that, although I won't do it again. Another performance of that kind, and you *will* be on your way home. At the moment you're Head of House and a school prefect as well.'

'Iain tells me he has told you about—about David.'

'So he has—and he told me he was going to tell you he'd told me. I think he has been most terribly concerned, Robin. But whether he ought to have discussed it with me, I hardly know. There are sad things among young people that older people can't really be much help over.'

Robin was silent for a moment, and I felt that it was by way of conveying the impression that he had been listening to a thoroughly feeble speech. Perhaps he had.

'You're only thinking of the fact that I'm fond of the kid,' he said. 'I expect that's just my bad luck—just as my father is bad luck. But you're no good. None of you lot are any good. You won't face up to what can happen in those places. That bloody Belsen! It's contemptible. I hate it, hate it! Fuck you all.' And Robin Hayes turned and walked out of the room.

So thus had the boy apologized. I was left in a condition which might conventionally be described as 'stunned'. But in fact it was a condition more complex, or merely confused, than that. There was an element of relief in it. Robin, it seemed to me, had tumbled abruptly from a *crise de nerfs* into a condition of positive nervous breakdown. However deplorable the state of affairs in School House (and I strongly suspected that Iain Macleod's highly coloured account of it had itself been influenced by Robin's rhetoric) what I had just been treated to was a sick boy's disproportionate reaction to a testing situation. It was also the reaction of a boy who had been plied with wine to the point of helpless drunkenness by an uncle whom I was increasingly disposed to view in a sinister light. But a sick Robin Hayes—and this was where my fugitive sense of relief came in—was a Robin Hayes who would become sane and well again. He was to be seen as ill—and illnesses run their course.

I had arrived at this facile and comforting view of the matter when, for the second time that day, I was summoned to the telephone.

'Pog.'

For a moment this conveyed nothing to me.

'Pog—it's Owen Marchmont.'

'Hallo,' I said. 'Hallo, Owen.'

'Are you alone?'

'Yes. Yes, I am.'

'Do your boys get newspapers?'

'Newspapers?' Not surprisingly, I was bewildered. 'Yes, of course. The senior ones have their own papers delivered to them in their studies, and I always see to it that there's a paper in the junior day-room. But why . . .?'

'That boy Hayes is still with you?'

'Yes, of course.' An indefinable foreboding assailed me. 'Is there bad news for him?'

'I suppose it's that. Anyway, you'd better get hold of him and let him have it before he comes across it in one of tomorrow's rags. His father has left us.'

'*Left* you? I don't understand.'

'This is an open prison, isn't it—heaven help us? Just walked out—you might say with his brief-case and his bowler hat and his umbrella.'

'Owen, surely that's madness? And he'll be picked up in no time?'

'Of course it is—in a way. And of course he will be, without doubt.'

'And then he'll be transferred to somewhere much less pleasant for the rest of his time?'

'He may be—but, you know, the system is extremely rum. I've ceased to think I'll ever understand it. But there it is. I'm deprived of the society of Mr Hayes, that distinguished legal luminary and former Carthusian. It's quite a blow.'

I realized that, to the Governor of Hutton Green, it *was* a blow; that it further undermined what faith in his institution he retained. I felt annoyed with Mr Hayes. Then I remembered Robin, and my annoyance turned to anger.

'The stupid old bastard!' I said. 'As it happens, his boy has a good deal of trouble on his plate already, just at present. This will be a bit more.'

'I'm sorry to hear that, Pog. But the kid mustn't take it too hard. It shows a certain spunk in his old dad—in a way.'

'It shows nothing of the kind.'

'If you'd been put in quod, Pog, and suddenly saw an open door in front of you . . .'

'All right, Owen—all right. Where do you think the chap will have made for? His unappealing wife in that cathedral city?'

'Perhaps so. But what about his son and Helmingham? Give me a call—there's a good fellow—if the door-bell rings and there he is in front of you.' Marchmont paused briefly. 'Sorry,' he said. 'It's got me a little rattled, really. I'll keep you informed, Pog. Goodbye.'

And the telephone went dead with a click.

Marchmont's news must be conveyed to Robin at once, and perceiving this made me realize that my relationship with the boy had now become almost an impossible one. It was all very well to tell myself he was sick; his behaviour, and the words with which he had left me, suggested a trouble better to be described as a personality change—if that expression didn't imply something with a character of permanence I wasn't prepared to accept. The disturbance, however radical for the moment, would pass as a brain-storm passes. Of this I remained convinced, but the conviction didn't make for less of awkwardness—really impossible awkwardness—in the short term. Sadly I had to confess to myself that there was no point (or none but the wretched Daviot aspect of the thing) in Robin Hayes remaining for another day at Helmingham. Nor, I found, did I want to summon him and attempt as sympathetically as possible to tell him of his father's stupid behaviour. He had, in effect, told me to get lost, and I had an irrational feeling that there would be an element of ungenerous retort in giving him such dismal information. In this demoralized condition I thought of Father Edwards, who was regarded throughout the school as the proper man to convey to a boy the fact of some sudden domestic tragedy. Mr Hayes's conduct wasn't quite of that order, but I didn't see why Edwards shouldn't be brought in. So I rang him up, explained as much of the situation as was necessary, and readily persuaded him to come over to Heynoe and seek out Robin Hayes at once.

It thus came about that I didn't see Robin again on that Sunday. Nor was he on view at breakfast on the Monday morning. This was no more than a mild irregularity, and although I thought of sending Iain Macleod to haul him out of bed (these two boys had bedrooms of their own, immediately adjoining the two junior dormitories; the other senior boys had what were called study-bedrooms) it seemed to me better not to fuss. Then at lunch-time a colleague rang me up to say that Hayes hadn't appeared at two classes, and as there hadn't been a chit about him he supposed he'd better let me know. I said something vague about the boy's having been seedy the day before, and put down the receiver. Within seconds the bell rang again and I was listening once more, to John Stafford's voice.

'Syson? I've had a note from Hayes.'

'From the boy's father, Head Master?' I supposed that Mr

Hayes had been employing his precariously achieved liberty to enter into correspondence with Stafford about his son.

'Of course not. From the boy himself. It enclosed a blank cheque to pay for the repair of your front door. He wasn't minded, he says, to hand it to you himself.'

'How very extraordinary.' Most of the senior boys had their own bank accounts, and it wasn't this turning up of another cheque in the affair that astonished me. It was the further evidence of Robin's complete alienation.

'Or to say goodbye.'

'To *what?*'

'He has departed, Syson. Had you happened to see a taxi leaving your own shattered door an hour ago, you might also have seen your Head Boy inside it.'

'I see.' I took hold of myself as I spoke—resolved, although for the moment almost shattered by this intelligence, to deal with it in a forthright and composed fashion. 'Perhaps—if in a graceless way—he has made a sensible enough decision. Oxford is in front of him, and his having come back to school wasn't working out too well. He was having difficulties.'

'So it appears—and that one of the difficulties goes by the name of Daviot. I hadn't been apprized of it.' And Stafford made one of his pauses. 'Of Hayes's departure in itself I'd not be disposed to take much account, Syson. But unfortunately he hasn't departed alone. He has taken Daviot—a very much younger boy—along with him.'

# VII

SO ROBIN HAYES and his father were both, in a sense, at large.
But there was a difference. Mr Hayes was already being hunted
for, and as soon as hand was laid upon him he would be locked
up. Robin had simply chosen to go upon his lawful occasions.
And although there was doubtless something equivocal about
his having chosen to take with him what Stafford had grimly
called 'a very much younger boy', no police officer or magistrate
would feel prompted to hasty action in face of the escapade. A
good deal would depend here on the attitude of David Daviot's
grandfather, the judge. But he, too, was unlikely to act in a hasty
way provoking public scandal. Nobody would want that—and
John Stafford would be particularly anxious to see the dubious
event kept out of what he was fond of calling, in the idiom of a
past age, the penny papers.

One question occupied my mind almost as soon as per-
turbation had a little subsided in it. Mr Hayes had left his
open prison, and his son had left what he had perhaps chosen to
regard as a similar institution, roughly speaking within twenty-
four hours of one another: Mr Hayes first, and Robin, along
with David, second. And Robin had known about Mr Hayes's
absconding from Hutton Green, since Father Edwards had
broken the news to him—or had so done if it had *been* news. For
there were two possibilities. Either father and son had for some
reason contrived to work in concert together, or Robin's action
had simply been triggered off by what Edwards had revealed to
him; Robin had been—in what was becoming a current
phrase—'destabilized'. There seemed to be no present means of
determining which of these interpretations of the situation was
the more probable.

Was any light to be shed on the mystery through a

consideration of Robin Hayes's character? Asking myself this question revealed to me the disconcerting fact that, until these current troubles, I had never done more than take a mild unreflecting pleasure in him. He had been an agreeable boy of whom it was easy to approve, and he had done a little more than adequately everything to lead him to his position of authority and general acceptance in the House. But what about this typically satisfactory English schoolboy in his family relations? That his father's disgrace had deeply wounded him I didn't doubt, but injured pride or even vanity could be a large component in this. There had been that hint of a grasping disposition embarrassing to his father's purse. And there had been what I had taken to be a certain hardness, or even cynicism, lurking in his attitude to the whole family disaster. But all this was ground which I had in a way mulled over already, and it really told me very little when thus considered again. I couldn't be sure, for example, that Robin's sudden bolting from Helmingham hadn't been prompted, at least in part, by a filial impulse to contact his father and make him see some saving sense. And he might have taken David Daviot with him—snatched from the horrors or presumed horrors of School House—from a not too clear-headed impulse to kill two laudable birds with one stone.

Jasper Tandem came into my head next, and I presently saw—or thought I saw—the significance of that cheque so brutally flourished at me as Iain Macleod hauled Robin off to bed. I knew it to be Jasper's cheque, and now saw it as given to the boy simply to finance the major folly by which we were confronted. Jasper Tandem, I decided, was precisely the wicked uncle that Robin and his sister had predicated. He had planned mischief, perhaps in some obscure fashion to his own advantage, more probably for the mere pleasure of unmotivated malice. Having thus brought an Iago-like figure into the picture I felt a momentary satisfaction—and then told myself I was wasting my time.

And time was passing. Tuesday morning came with still no word of the fugitives. Deciding to confer with Tim Taplow, I walked over to School House, and was admitted by Jubb. Jubb was among the properties distinguishing School House from the rest of us, being the only manservant of a comparable sort at Helmingham. Originally a handyman of humble degree, he had studied the comportment of film and television butlers with such diligence as virtually to transform himself into that sort of person, so that eventually it had become necessary that appropriate duties should be devised for him.

Jubb announced with gravity that Mr Taplow was teaching, but might be expected back in ten or fifteen minutes, and I allowed myself to be ceremoniously ushered into his study to wait for him. There I found another prospective visitor. Johncock—Clive Johncock, as I understood him to be—was standing by the window, impatiently jingling the small change in a trouser-pocket.

'Oh, hallo,' Johncock said. 'Have you dropped in to discuss the *Entführung*?'

'The what?'

'*Aus dem Serail*, you know. Mozart.'

'Certainly Mozart.' I must have looked at this ill-mannered young man (as I no doubt conceived him to be) with disfavour.

'Well, the elopement has taken place, hasn't it? I've just heard about it. But I'm not quite sure of the seraglio. According to some reports, School House has turned into a bit of a brothel. An exaggeration, perhaps.'

'Do I understand, Johncock, that you've come in to discuss with Taplow the disappearance of a couple of our boys—Hayes and Daviot?'

'Not specifically that, although it all hitches up. Taplow, it seems, has been worrying over his control of this dump, and has asked me if I'd think of moving in and lending a hand.'

'Ah, yes. He mentioned the idea to me, as a matter of fact, on Saturday. Are you going to agree?'

'I think not. Why should I my unhoused free condition put into circumscription and confine? I rather imagine I've come in to utter a polite No. If I can utter anything politely, that is.' Johncock glanced at me in a kind of innocent mischief which I didn't find disagreeable. 'But of course the rape of the infant Daviot is quite a facer—for Taplow as well as for yourself. So perhaps it's an occasion for all good men to rally round. And, come to think of it, I'd save quite a bit on the perks.'

'If I were you, Clive'—for I knew I ought to establish friendly relations with this young mathematician—'I'd give yourself a little time to think, before deciding one way or the other. I'm sure you'd be a help to the Taplows. But in some ways your position might be awkward. Don't you agree?'

'Of course I do, Robert. And I don't think it's a plan that would have come into the head of a man with a natural instinct for housemastering. But that just makes deciding more difficult, as a matter of fact. Hallo, here he comes. But not, one imagines, feeling exactly the conquering hero.'

Tim Taplow's footsteps had made themselves heard in the hall, and in a moment he was in the room. As one might have predicted, he bore a harassed look, and for a moment he occupied himself with tugging off his gown rather in the manner of a Heracles endeavouring to cope with Nessus' shirt.

'Robert,' he said, '—I was going to contact you. I'm glad you've come. If it isn't the very devil! Oh, Clive too— Good!'

'I'll drop in another time,' Johncock said. 'Or give me a ring, and I'll canter across.'

'No, no!' What I judged to be a surprising and proper tact on Johncock's part seemed merely to agitate Taplow further. 'Stay where you are. You can probably help us. Robert—that's right?'

'Yes, of course.' I could hardly have expressed dissent, even had I wanted to. But in fact I was coming round to the view that Clive Johncock was a useful—if occasionally graceless—man. He was younger than Taplow and very much younger than myself: I had a feeling that he might have a surer sense than either of us of the mind of the more youthful still. 'Three are better than two in any council of war.'

This was not a particularly meaningful remark, but Johncock seemed pleased by it, and promptly sat down on the most comfortable chair in the room.

'I'm the outsider,' he said. 'It's my rôle. Particularly *vis-à-vis*

Messrs Hayes and Daviot. At my sort of school, you know, the boys don't fall in love with one another—or they very rarely do. I don't at all know why not, but it's certainly the case. So here's one of the points at which public schools score.'

'*Score?*' Taplow said, plainly startled.

'It's maturing, if you ask me. Do you remember us talking, not all that long ago, about earlier maturation among adolescents nowadays? Well, out in the world, so to speak, it can be of a raw and pretty hideous sort. Wasn't I saying something about sex in the telly culture? I ought to have been, because I think about it quite a lot: sex as simply an arena for predatory grab. But in places like this, variously absurd as they are, what is undoubtedly sexual feeling of a sort has scope to express itself, and test its muscle, in a more decently human way. God knows what the thing can be called. One has to use "romantic friendship", or some such corny phrase. But there's something to be said for it, so far as nudging kids in the direction of civilised adult feeling and behaviour is concerned.'

'I see,' Taplow said seriously—although he was no doubt as surprised as I was by this fresh facet of Johncock's thinking, and may also have been wondering whether Johncock was quite the man for the job he had been proposing. 'But it doesn't alter the fact that what we're confronted with at the moment is a pretty kettle of fish. What are those two runaways up to? Educating each other for a mature citizenship? Don't make me laugh.'

'Quite precisely what they're up to isn't all that important.' It was with some surprise that I heard myself break in with this. 'The essential point is, Tim, that the occasion of their flight seems to hitch on to what Clive has been talking about. Hayes—who has certainly been thrown quite off balance by one thing or another—believes himself to be rescuing little Daviot from Heaven knows what, here in School House. I think Hayes has received some almost vicious prompting from an irresponsible uncle—but that's by the way. The main fact is that a kind of chivalrous impulse appears to be at work. What sort of boy is being rescued from the dragon I scarcely know.'

'Little Daviot,' Taplow said a shade defensively, 'isn't all that bad. Silly, no doubt.'

'And stage-struck? Father Edwards tells me he's that. It may be a factor in their plans. Daviot may believe immediate stardom awaits him, if he can just get away from Helmingham.'

'But what about Hayes?' Johncock asked sharply. 'Can he be dotty enough to believe that?'

'I don't think he can.' I was in fact certain of this at once. 'But now there's another thing. My Hayes is not the only Hayes on the run.'

'Robert, what the devil do you mean by that?' It was plain that Taplow was irritated again.

'Hayes's father is in gaol, you remember. Or, rather, he has been in gaol. He walked out of it the day before yesterday. So far as I know, he's still at large.'

'Do you mean,' Johncock demanded, 'that he and his son have made a rendezvous, and with young Daviot to keep them company?'

'It does seem a possibility. I had Edwards break to the boy the news of his father's foolish behaviour, and Robin then seems to have packed up at once and departed from us. It's conceivable that his father's act was something the boy had reason to expect. But I incline to the view that it was just a final stroke toppling his remaining good sense.'

'We're getting nowhere,' Taplow suddenly exploded. 'Bloody nowhere! And meanwhile the story is running through the whole school?'

'It will certainly be doing that,' I said. 'Thank goodness half term is only a few days away.' At Helmingham, I ought to explain, this particular half term in the year is quite a considerable affair, the entire school dispersing for a week. 'There will be a bit of a breather in that.'

'There will be six hundred boys let loose on the land,' Johncock said. 'Not to speak of small contingents going to Saudi Arabia and Bahrain. And all with this story on their eager young lips. Well may we bless half term.'

I hadn't thought of this, and for a moment we all fell silent. Then suddenly the door of Taplow's study was flung open by Jubb—a Jubb who bellowed at the top of his voice: 'The Honourable Mr Justice Daviot!'

And thus the fugitive David's grandfather arrived on our scene.

It was like being called upon to be upstanding in court. But the visitor showed neither annoyance nor amusement at Jubb's performance, advancing upon Taplow and shaking hands in silence. He seemed quite as old as even English judges are allowed to be, and he was handsome in a heavy way. Still having a fairly clear picture of David Daviot in my head, I tried to imagine Sir Henry at his grandson's age. Was the handsomeness of the one distinguishably related to the beauty of the other? Naturally I found no answer to this—and now Taplow was introducing us.

'Mr Syson,' Taplow said. 'Mr Syson is the housemaster'—and he hesitated for a moment—'of the boy Hayes.'

I didn't much care for this, since Taplow might almost have been saying, 'of the wretched defendant'. But Sir Henry shook hands and murmured something polite.

'And this,' Taplow went on, 'is Mr Johncock, an assistant master, who is entirely in our confidence.' I didn't greatly care for this either, since it might have been a formula for presenting a superior kind of clerk. And Sir Henry said nothing, gave Johncock a bow, and then a brief straight look. Whereupon Johncock, with what I thought admirable composure, gave a bow in his turn, said something inaudible to Taplow, and left the room.

'And now,' Sir Henry Daviot said with a quite indefinable largeness of courtesy as he allowed himself to be ushered into a chair, 'we can put our heads together over this unfortunate episode. We can try—if the expression isn't too portentous for such a vagary—to probe its occasion.' He paused on this. 'One wonders,' he went on, 'whether the boys have run away to sea—whether as stowaways or as cook's apprentices. The adventure stories used to make it out in that way.'

I was surprised by this almost trivializing remark. It seemed out of character. It seemed to be this even although the judge's character was something I knew nothing about. But I recalled telling myself that it would be the instinct of anyone in his position to be chary of inflating a delicate family affair. Not that the old man hadn't acted promptly enough. For here he was, post-haste from London, in his grandson's housemaster's study. I wondered whether he had called on John Stafford first.

'I needn't tell you, sir, that we are all deeply concerned—and myself in particular—over what has happened.' Having begun, very properly, with this, Taplow promptly took the initiative in asking questions, and I realized with relief that he was going to show up well. 'Has David been in correspondence with you throughout the term so far?'

'Certainly. The customary weekly letters, Mr Taplow. There has been little of anything that hinted distress in them. But there are matters about which letters from school are prescriptively uninformative. Or am I insufficiently up to date? My own schooldays are rather far behind me.'

'One can scarcely generalize, Sir Henry. Judging from some letters that I get from parents, there are boys who send home a regular bill of indictment every week. Robert, would you agree?'

'Certainly,' I said. 'But I'd guess it to be minority behaviour. Public school education is appallingly costly nowadays, and probably four boys out of five are conscious that their parents are making considerable sacrifices to manage it. So they make their reports home as favourable as possible.'

Sir Henry inclined his head slightly. Previously, he had been turning it from one to the other of us with an air of greater attention than I felt we warranted. He had only to listen with sufficient patience—his attitude seemed to imply—and truth would emerge, whether we liked it or not.

'What about the summer holidays?' It was perhaps with a shade less of confidence that Taplow thus took the initiative anew. One doesn't—he might have been reflecting—ask a judge questions. Contrariwise. 'Did David offer any suggestion then that he was unhappy at school?'

'Had he done so, Mr Taplow, it is quite certain that I should have inquired into the matter rigorously. But there was nothing of the sort. It is true that I saw less of him that I would have wished. He was active over his own concerns—and particularly in the way of theatre-going. I saw to it that it was commonly with an older companion.'

'He is very taken up with the stage, is he not? And has shown signs of possessing some talent as an actor. One idea already in the air is that his leaving us so abruptly is conceivably connected with precocious and obviously unrealistic theatrical ambitions.' Taplow paused on this. But Sir Henry, who was all large attention, said nothing. So Taplow went on. 'Yet I'm afraid—and I mustn't conceal it for a moment—that there is some reason to believe that your grandson has indeed been unhappy here in School House for some time. There have been instances of bullying, and perhaps of other forms of misbehaviour, which I am ashamed to say I have been too slow to spot and jump on. I am doing something positive about it now.' (This, I supposed, was a reference to the proposal to recruit Johncock in the fight against juvenile crime.) 'But, so far as David is concerned, that may be a matter of locking the stable door a little on the late side.'

This was, perhaps, a little on the trite side, and David's grandfather received it in silence. I felt it was my turn to speak.

'And that, Sir Henry, is where my boy—a very senior boy—comes in. He has formed a friendship with David—a warm friendship of a schoolboy character—and seems to have arrived at an exaggerated view of your grandson's sufferings. Hayes, in fact, has been thrown a little off his balance—and I suspect, moreover, that he has been receiving bad advice from an uncle. The result has been his removing David from the school in a kind of rescue operation. It is absurd and no doubt reprehensible. But there has been some spark of honourable feeling in it.'

'Mr Syson, if the facts turn out to be as you state, your verdict may be valid enough. For then what we are confronted with is mere juvenile folly which can be soon mended. So I hope you are right.'

This seemed a judicious and temperate speech, and I wondered why I wasn't quite satisfied with it. Then I saw that there lurked in it an odd proviso. Whether my facts were right or not, what could there possibly be in what Johncock had dubbed the *Entführung* that the term 'juvenile folly' wouldn't adequately cover? Asking myself this, I thought I saw what must be in our elderly visitor's head. If the elopement, like most actual elopements, was as well as a rescue a prelude to specific sexual activity, this would be something beyond the bounds of mere folly in his mind. It was a way of thinking with which I had no great sympathy—observation having confirmed me in the view that with adolescent boys more harm is done by creating an uproar over such spontaneous affairs than by letting them run their brief course to a conclusion. But perhaps Her Majesty's judges were more or less obliged to subscribe to a different opinion. And of course when I was myself aware of anything of the sort going on I was always in considerable anxiety about it, since it could put careers at hazard and occasion acute distress in a boy's home.

'Whatever the precise facts may be,' Sir Henry was saying, 'we have to address ourselves to the task of running our young friends to earth—or to sea, if they do happen to have engaged themselves as cabin-boys. We need not, I feel, be in a hurry to call in the police, or publicize the affair in any way. There is no substantial sense in which harm is likely to have come to them. At the worst they may have met with a road-accident, and be in hospital with broken limbs and no disposition to identify themselves. Even so, matters will straighten themselves out.' The judge paused on this, and I had a momentary sense that he didn't quite believe what he had said. There was, in fact, some deep agitation hidden in him. 'We must bestir ourselves, nevertheless. I wonder what money they have. Not, I imagine, very much. I certainly don't believe in giving a child like David a great deal.'

'I'm not sure about that,' I said. 'Hayes has his own bank account, and I have reason to believe he was given a cheque for what may have been a substantial amount by an uncle only a couple of days ago.'

'The irresponsible uncle,' Taplow asked, 'that you believe to be a nigger in the woodpile?'

'Yes, Tim. Tandem. Mrs Hayes's wealthy brother.'

Sir Henry, for the first time since he had sat down, stirred in his chair. For a moment, I believe, his attention had lapsed from us. And it was oddly, somehow, that he now spoke.

'That name,' he said. 'A common enough name, I suppose.'

'Tandem?' I repeated in surprise. 'I never heard the word as a surname before.'

'No, no—Hayes. I mean Hayes.' The judge was now sitting stiffly in his chair, and the brief look he directed on me made me feel much like a man in a dock. 'Mr Syson,' he said sternly, 'is information that I ought to have received being withheld from me?'

'Most certainly not, Sir Henry.' Although for a moment angry and confused by this abrupt hostile treatment, the explanation of it was clear to me at once. It had simply not entered my head that our visitor was unaware of having sent to prison the father of my Head of House. But why—unless he had indeed made a call on John Stafford—should he know anything of the kind? 'I must apologize,' I went on. 'I've been taking something for granted about your bearings in this affair. Robin Hayes, the boy who has gone off with David, does happen to be the son of a man you had to deal with not many months ago. A case of embezzlement by a country solicitor.'

'Well I'm blessed!' Taplow said. I had already told him of this odd fact, but he had clearly forgotten about it. 'It certainly adds a touch of irony, or something of that sort, to the picture.'

'No doubt it may be viewed in that light, Mr Taplow.' The judge somehow contrived to make this colourless remark sound particularly courteous. I told myself that he had regained his composure—and the reflection made me realize that he must momentarily have lost it. What could account for this, I didn't know. Perhaps it was merely that there was an additional humiliation in the fact that the companion his grandson had chosen to bolt from school with was the son of a convicted criminal. But now it occurred to me that there was another piece of information that David's grandfather should have.

'Perhaps I ought to mention,' I said, 'that Hayes's father, who has been in a place called Hutton Green, has absconded from it. I had the news from the Governor—he happens to be a schoolfellow of mine—the day before yesterday, and I had it passed on to the boy at once. It seems possible that it was the final prompting to his own departure from Helmingham.'

'With my grandson.'

These words arrested me—precisely because they were otiose and made no contribution to our discussion. And Sir Henry Daviot, one could see, was not a man for idle reiteration. Again I had the sense of his being upset. The mere fact of the identity of Robin's father had startled him, and now it was almost as if he had for a moment been positively alarmed on being told of the convicted man's senseless behaviour. Perhaps it was no more than a kind of reflex action. Perhaps judges and magistrates regularly experienced a brief sensation of the kind on learning that somebody they had sent to prison had broken out and was on the prowl again. The same reaction mightn't attach to the mere knowledge that such a man had finished his regular sentence. It would be an irrational feeling in either case, since released criminals, although sometimes prompted to take it out of witnesses and accomplices who have offended their sense of justice, seldom if ever have a go at the beaks who have judged their case.

However all that might be, Sir Henry was quickly composed again, and had now turned to address me with the habitual formal politeness of the bench.

'Mr Taplow and I,' he said, 'have of course discussed my grandson's character on former occasions. I have, I believe, a fairly clear view of David—although it is undoubtedly true that small boys can pack surprises. Some of the most astonishing things I have ever heard in court have come from juveniles who could scarcely get their noses above the witness box. That is by the way. Of the boy Hayes I know nothing at all. I wonder, Mr Syson, whether you would be good enough to afford me some view of him?'

It was a reasonable request, and if it disconcerted me this must have been because it further conjured up in Tim Taplow's study something like the atmosphere of a law court. I did my best to give a fair picture of the unfortunate Robin, and when I had finished Sir Henry made me a grave bow and thanked me for having been a great help to him. It was exactly as if I had been a very junior counsel who had been hopefully rambling before him.

'I wonder,' he then said blandly, 'What the boy's contemporaries think of him—and whether perhaps any of them has been in his confidence? Has he a particularly close friend in Heynoe, Mr Syson?'

'His fellow-prefect, a boy called Macleod, is certainly his closest friend.'

'Then I wonder whether Macleod might be sent for?'

This was decidedly taking charge of things. But again the request was a reasonable one, given the unfortunate situation in which we found ourselves.

'Certainly we can talk to Macleod,' I said. 'But, if you will excuse me, I'll go and fetch him myself. Where friends are concerned, one wants to avoid the effect of a summons.'

Sir Henry received this with a nod as of cordial agreement, but he mayn't have been too pleased. Nor was I quite contented with myself. The Hayes affair was turning me prickly. I had come thoroughly to dislike Mr Tandem. I wasn't exactly disliking the judge. But I did feel that there was some still-hidden facet to him which might prove awkward at any time. Saying something about being back in ten minutes, I left the room. Taplow and his visitor, I told myself, could have another chat about David's character.

I glanced at my watch, and saw that I might have to yank Macleod out of class by means of a messenger and a chit—a procedure always to avoid if one could. But it wasn't so. Macleod had a free hour, and I found him in the library.

'Iain,' I said, 'two things. First, this small catastrophe makes you acting Head of House. Second, Daviot's grandfather is here in Mr Taplow's study. He'd be grateful if you'd come and talk to him.'

'Isn't he a judge or something?' My new Head of House was properly wary.

'Yes, and distinctly judicial as well. But he is the brat's stand-in for a father, and we have to go along with his efforts to sort things out. So I'd be grateful if you'd come and lend a hand.'

'A hand—yes. But I don't know about a head as well.' Macleod had set out with me at once. 'I'm a bit bewildered, I mean, about the whole thing. What does this judge-person think is happening to his grandson? Suffering a fate worse than death?'

'I imagine so. What do *you* think? I have to ask you, because I suspect *he* will.'

'I don't think it will have been what was in Robin's mind.'

'I agree.' It seemed to me that Macleod had produced a notably well-judged reply. 'Mr Johncock is making a silly if harmless joke about an elopement, and other people may see it that way, too. But Robin at least wasn't positively planning a seduction. We can express our conviction as to that.'

Macleod nodded, but said nothing. He was clearly turning over in his mind the problem of giving some sort of testimony about his friend. We walked on in silence, and had reached the gate of School House when I became aware of Miss Sparrow advancing towards us on the footpath with a businesslike shopping-basket on her arm. A sudden inspiration came to me.

'Hallo,' I said. 'Iain and I are going in here to talk to the grandfather of the Daviot boy in Tim's study. Come with us.'

'Would you say that Mr Taplow is inviting me?' Halted at the garden gate, Miss Sparrow was amused.

'Don't dither. It *is* a mess, and we all have to pile in. And on anything connected with Heynoe House you are an impeccable expert witness.'

So Miss Sparrow joined us. I was pleased about this. There were aspects of the boys' life in Heynoe which she knew more about than I did. And it was in my mind that the presence of a lady might deter Sir Henry Daviot from expatiating on that worse-than-death conjecture.

He did at least express himself as gratified by Miss Sparrow's accession to our numbers, although what he really thought about it, I don't know. Certainly his interest was immediately centred on Iain.

'Mr Macleod,' he said, 'I hope you don't mind my having suggested to your housemaster that we have a talk?'

'No, sir.'

'I understand that Robin Hayes and you are friends and enjoy a good deal of one another's confidence—as one might expect from the joint responsibility you hold in Heynoe.' Sir Henry paused on this. He was being very much the old public school boy himself. 'Now, Macleod, it may very well be that in discussing his affairs with you Hayes touched on matters which you don't feel at liberty to repeat.'

'No. I don't know that he did.'

'I must of course respect any reticence that you may feel proper.'

'I don't think, sir, I have any occasion to be reticent. And I've just said so.'

'Very well.' The judge gave every appearance of approving this stiff reply—even greeting it with one of his grave bows. 'And of course we must be quite clear that your friend's departing from Helmingham is in itself his own affair. He has come of age and is his own master. Just as you yourself are.'

'Yes.'

'But he has taken my grandson away with him: a boy who had his fourteenth birthday a few weeks ago. You will see that there is a difficulty there.'

'It can be called that, I suppose.'

'Naturally I am very much concerned, and feel it urgently necessary to discover where Robin and David have betaken themselves. You understand that?'

'Of course I do. And I want to know myself.'

'You have no idea where they have gone to? Nothing that Robin has said . . .?'

'No—nothing. He didn't say a thing. Even when he was blind drunk he didn't. It has been as ugly a surprise to me as to you.'

'I see.' Robin's blind drunkenness must have been a fresh increment of information for the judge, but he gave no sign of taking account of it. 'Then what about a *guess*, Macleod?' The judge brought this forward whimsically. 'Where would you say, quite at a venture, that Hayes and my grandson are heading for now?'

'Morocco, perhaps. Or California.'

'Dear me! But isn't getting to such places a matter of considerable expense?'

'Of course it is. But there was that cheque from his uncle. Robin *said* nothing. But he did show it to me. Or flip it at me, rather—just as he flipped it at Mr Syson. And I happened to see the amount. It was for a thousand pounds.'

This produced a second's silence. We were conferring, it must be remembered, a number of years ago, when a thousand pounds still seemed a very large sum of money. Then Tim Taplow spoke.

'Is this the wicked uncle again?' he asked. 'Jasper Hayes?'

'Not a Hayes,' I said. 'I've told you. Tandem. He's on the mother's side. Jasper Tandem.'

My words had—at least for a perceptible moment—a startling effect. For the second time during this unusual conference a species of rigor appeared to have afflicted Sir Henry Daviot. He had stiffened as he sat. On the first occasion both these names had been uttered, but it had been that of Hayes that had produced this odd phenomenon. This time it had been the name of poor Mr Hayes's bad-hat brother-in-law. What to make of such behaviour, I didn't at all know. But, just as before, Sir Henry was quickly at ease again. For some seconds, indeed, he said nothing—but his silence was of the forensic sort that suggests that the form of some particularly penetrating questions is being carefully thought out.

'Macleod,' he asked, 'would you say that Robin is an impulsive lad, prone sometimes to act rashly and upon insufficient consideration of the consequences of what he is about?'

'He is impulsive—yes.'

'What happens when he sees he's on a wrong tack? Does he turn right-about and return to base again?'

'No. Typically or characteristically, that is, he's somebody who still drives ahead.'

'A stiff-necked boy?'

'I don't know about that. I think the expression is a disagreeable one.' Macleod delivered himself of this rebuke quite calmly. 'I'd say that Robin is a rebel. I wish I was.'

'Do you, indeed?'

'This is a very good school. But in a way any such place is a kind of forcing house for conformities. And his instinct is against that.'

'I see. Well, making off with a young companion to California is certainly not conforming behaviour. And you think that, having once bought the tickets, Robin would see to it that they both went on board?'

'I do think that.'

A brief silence followed upon these exchanges, and I told myself that Macleod was not without a certain romantic admiration for his friend. The person who next spoke was Miss Sparrow.

'I don't think I agree with Iain,' she said. 'What he says about Robin's character is true in a way. Only it doesn't allow for a considerable amount of simple common sense in the boy's make up.'

'This is extremely interesting, Miss Sparrow.' The judge was at his most courteous. 'Would you be inclined to assert that there has been a considerable amount of common sense in the boy's decamping with my grandson?'

'Most certainly.'

'Can you expand on that? It would be of great assistance to me.'

'It doesn't need much expanding, Sir Henry. Robin believed, rightly or wrongly, that David was having a very unhappy time in this House. So he took him away from it. I don't say that a good deal of excitement and romantic feeling wasn't generated by the situation—and possibly fuelled by that most injudicious thousand pounds. But I believe that, almost at once, common sense would win the day.'

'And with what result, Miss Sparrow?'

'Robin would simply take David straight home, and perhaps hope to discuss the situation, Sir Henry, with yourself.'

'It is a comfortable view.' The judge contrived to offer this at once politely and grimly. 'But if David had been brought straight home I shouldn't be here now.'

And now Sir Henry Daviot was on his feet. With both hands he made the slightest of quasi-papal gestures—the action of a man accustomed to having the most slender indications of his pleasure obeyed. Our conference was over, and he was inviting us to disperse.

'I am most grateful to you, all four,' he said. 'We have had a most useful discussion, and now I must keep an appointment with the Head Master.' He then shook hands with us, beginning with Miss Sparrow, and without the assistance of Jubb departed from School House.

I went back to Heynoe and endeavoured to apply my mind to correcting Greek unseens. At the end of an hour the telephone rang.

'Stafford,' said John Stafford's voice.

'Yes, Head Master.'

'You've had that old man Daviot with you?'

'Not exactly that. I was with Taplow in School House, and Daviot was shown in on us. Later, there were Miss Sparrow and my second prefect as well. We had an odd sort of discussion about this thing.'

'An odd sort of discussion. Was Daviot odd too?'

'Odd?' This disconcerted me a little. 'Once or twice he made me slightly uneasy. I don't quite know why.'

'You didn't feel he ought to be locked up?'

'Good heavens, no!'

'Then the man contrived to go completely off his head between Taplow's house and mine. About a hundred and fifty yards, Syson. Just who is going mad next? How do you feel yourself?'

This was the awkward and uncharacteristic gamesomeness into which I recalled Stafford as sometimes dropping when he was upset.

'Tolerably normal,' I said. 'Just what happened?'

'It was all quite in order at the start. I even told myself he wasn't as bothered as I'd have expected, considering this alarming carrying off of his grandson.'

'Perhaps, Head Master, we ought to avoid describing it just like that. There's no evidence at all that David Daviot has departed from school unwillingly. Indeed, the initiative may conceivably have been his.'

'A valid point, Syson. Well, as I say, the man was perfectly sensible until we got on the business of the senior Hayes having bolted from quod—and then this other bolt immediately following at Helmingham. That seemed to touch something off, and he suddenly declared that it had been a concerted move; that father and son had been in collusion.'

'But I've debated that myself. Surely it's a tenable view, although an unlikely one.'

'Quite so. It's much more probable that the father's flight simply further upset the son and put the same notion of making a bolt of it into his head. But Daviot asserted his conviction in a most intemperate fashion. And then there was that disagreeable fellow Tandem, and his precious cheque. Daviot positively gibbered at the mention of him—I can't think why. Finally, he came back to your Robin Hayes and produced what I take to be a stroke of straight dottiness. He said, "I punished his father, didn't I? Now he and his father between them are out to punish my grandson". And I rather think he muttered something to the effect that Uncle Tandem was in on the plot as well. It's nonsense, isn't it?'

'I doubt whether we can be quite certain of that, Head Master. There's something malicious about Tandem—and I don't at all know what else there mayn't be as well. But there could be a paranoiac streak in that elderly judge.'

'That's the word I've been putting to it in my own head, Syson. And the thing was only the more alarming because it went as suddenly as it had arrived. Daviot took his leave of me in an entirely composed way, and with some sensible remarks on tracing the truants. It was almost as if his weird turn had been a product of dissociation, if that's what it's called. The long and the short of it is that this eminent judge is in an unstable state, to say the least, and may go over the top with stuff discrediting the school. So the sooner we get the affair cleared up, the better.'

I concurred in this sentiment, and John Stafford rang off. What I didn't quite go along with was the implication—which I thought I had detected in his tone—that the clearing up was entirely my responsibility.

# VIII

WITH HALF TERM came a week's freedom from both school routine and the always slightly more harassing affairs of Heynoe House. But as I watched my boys pile into their coaches or family cars I felt almost reluctant to part with them, since the problem they left me with became only the more oppressive.

Alarmingly by this time, nothing had been heard of our two absentees. Less alarmingly, perhaps, but even more unaccountably, nothing had been heard of the runaway Mr Hayes either. Owen Marchmont had again rung me up about his vanished guest, seemingly out of a not very rational persuasion that the man was likely to turn up at Helmingham at any moment in quest of his son. Not that Marchmont wasn't entirely rational about the general state of play. The failure to recapture Mr Hayes was something totally against expectation. Professional criminals, once they were over a prison wall, not infrequently eluded discovery for weeks, months, sometimes even years. But that was because a whole highly-organized underworld was waiting to receive them—quick, indeed, to make it a point of honour to take considerable risks to protect a man on the run. An outsider like poor Mr Hayes, strayed into prison with no credentials in the way of habitual wrong-doing, hadn't on any reasonable reckoning the ghost of a chance of spending so much as a single night at liberty. Marchmont seemed to think that he was probably dead; that he had fallen off a cliff into the sea or been swallowed by a quicksand. Alternatively, he might have ineptly slithered down a derelict mine shaft or clambered up a hopelessly decayed ladder into an abandoned silo, and be by now slowly perishing of thirst and hunger. Marchmont was really upset by these speculations.

'Tough on the chap's wife,' he said. 'Tiresome woman, but I'm sorry for her. Police more or less on the doorstep and among the gooseberry-bushes right round the clock. A particularly unseemly thing, I'd say, in the shadow of a cathedral. But unavoidable, you see. The blighter might bend his steps homewards at any time.'

'I wish the boy would, Owen.'

'The boy? Ah, yes—but that's different. No great need to worry about *him*. He's in possession of some money I suppose?'

'Hardly a doubt of it. Perhaps something over a thousand pounds.'

'Good lord! Well, good luck to him. He's entitled to go where he pleases, I imagine.'

'But not, surely, to take young Daviot, the judge's grandson, along with him.'

'I don't know about that, Pog—I don't know at all. Of course old Daviot is entitled to exercise his custody of his ward when they locate him. But meanwhile I rather doubt whether young Hayes is in any way breaking the law in accepting David— that's his name, isn't it?—as a travelling companion. Of course I'm interested in the boys, all the same. And there is now a police hunt for them, you know—if only because of the chance that they've joined up with your Robin's dad.'

'To come back to the mum, Owen—of course I've been in correspondence with her, and so has our Head Master. It must all be dreadfully worrying to her, and she is bound to feel that we have in some way failed her over her boy. But she doesn't show up to advantage with pen and paper, poor woman, and I think I ought to drive over and see her—particularly as I have a few clear days ahead of me. It seems the proper thing.'

'Ah, yes—the proper thing.' Marchmont, demonstrably a man much given to perpending the proper thing himself, repeated the phrase with a tiresome effect of mild amusement. But then he approved at once. 'Sound plan,' he said. 'You may pick up something helpful that has eluded the local bobbies. And, by the way, isn't there a daughter? I'd try to contact her, if I were you, without making too much of it. It's possible she has a line at least on the boys. A sister is sometimes closer to a lad than his parents are. Or so I'd suppose. I was an only child myself.'

'I'll try to do that, Owen.' For a moment I had been inclined to resent this suggestion—rather as if it would be turning me into a police spy. But something in my schoolfellow's tone as he spoke these last words brought it into my mind that he was a lonely man—and like myself a bachelor whose main contacts were with charges who of necessity stood rather remote from him. 'I'll let you hear of any impression I arrive at,' I said. 'You know, I did enjoy running into you so unexpectedly at your blessed Hutton Green. It was fun.'

'So it was. And—I say!—I must be pretty well on your route to and from the formidable Mrs H. Won't you drop in—either for a meal or a drink, as the hour suggests?'

'Thank you. Yes, I will.'

And when I had rung off I wrote at once to Mrs Hayes, asking permission to call on her. That, too, was no doubt the proper thing.

She responded by telephone on the following morning, thus making up in promptitude for a marked lack of cordiality apparent in her tone. But this reflection struck me at once as unjust. The woman had other things to think about than suggesting herself as a gracious, let alone grateful, prospective hostess. On the telephone she more or less said as much, informing me several times that she was in a very difficult situation. I reflected that so, of course, was her husband, and very possibly her son as well. But my sense of this she no doubt took for granted.

Driving across a couple of counties next day, I found myself thinking less of any conversation with Mrs Hayes ahead of me than of a short talk with Miss Sparrow before she had departed on a few days' holiday in what I conjectured to be naval circles. She had done little more than repeat with emphasis the opinion she had expressed at our meeting with David Daviot's grandfather. Robin Hayes might be liable to act impulsively and under the influence of romantic feeling. But the boy possessed a great deal of common sense which would almost at once assert itself following upon any rash action. And this ought to have resulted—Miss Sparrow was insistent—in his taking David almost straight home.

I had acknowledged that I felt considerable cogency in this view, but had pointed out to my Matron that a thousand pounds in a boy's pocket can be unsettling—and the more so if the gift of it be accompanied by deftly malicious prompting to adventure on the part of an older man.

'No doubt,' Miss Sparrow had said. 'But I still find the present situation unaccountable. I find Robin's silence unaccountable. I know he left Heynoe after speaking quite outrageously to yourself. But I'd expect him to make somebody—Iain Macleod, perhaps—a sign. I find myself almost afraid of there having been some disaster, even some crime. Robin manages to cash that enormous cheque . . .'

'He'd hardly need to do that if it had become his intention simply to take David home.'

'That's true.' Miss Sparrow had been put momentarily at a stand by my comment. 'But suppose he does. One can feel something vulnerable about it. And particularly if there has been any sort of rendezvous with his father. We don't know what sort of company Mr Hayes may have got himself into. Much less respectable than the company at Hutton Green, it may be.'

I had judged this apprehensiveness on the part of the robust Miss Sparrow surprising—even more surprising, somehow, than Owen Marchmont on the theme of mine shafts and silos. Now, as I drove between frosty hedgerows and over patches of snow (for the mild weather had departed and winter was pouncing on us), I found my mind turning to fantasy in a manner fairly to be described as alien to my temperament. I started imagining, quite weirdly, whole snow-fields traversed by wandering footprints, with here and there a dark splodge of blood thrown in. I conjured up police dogs—bloodhounds rather than any more realistic modern species—hunting down horrors not the less intimidating because only vaguely conceived. This curious indiscipline didn't last very long, but it suggested a nervous condition I didn't at all care for. It was with considerable relief that I eventually arrived in the suburbs of Uptoncester.

The small cathedral city, setting for the unspectacular wrong-doing of the elder Hayes, was then, and still is, a very undisturbed sort of place. There had been, indeed, an attempt to pitch a certain amount of light industry on its outskirts. But as this was mainly concerned with the manufacture of television sets and various electrical contraptions of domestic utility more efficiently produced in Italy or even the Far East, no permanent change was effected. The abortive 'industrial estate' was an unfrequented wilderness of empty warehouses and crumbling workshops of singularly depressing aspect. The city remained preponderantly a quiet haven of upper middle-class life, populated by the sort of people, it may be said, who send sons to schools like Helmingham. At Uptoncester anyone from Helmingham ought to feel at home.

On this occasion I felt not so much at home as—it may be said—sedated. The Georgian terraces—although a little post-Georgian and slightly stunted or anaemic as a result—were as suggestive of an ordered if undistinguished society as was the answering near-uniformity of garb among the persons neither hurrying nor loitering before them. Everything requiring paint was properly painted; the trees and shrubs, appropriately disposed, showed in their present bare condition as having been attentively lopped and clipped; a notable proportion of the shops displayed wares of superior quality. It was not an environment in which such peculations as Mr Hayes had achieved could have operated to any injurious extent. I fell into that frame of mind comfortably described as seeing things in their true proportions. Even the behaviour of Robin Hayes, although to be deprecated, came down to his having departed with a friend only a little prematurely in relation to our accustomed half-term dispersion. All this was perhaps of temporary effect, comparable to that produced by a dose of valium. But I was grateful for it as I identified and drew up before my destination.

My ring was answered by a uniformed housemaid, a circumstance carrying alike a sense of time-lag and the information that the Hayes family disaster had not yet been productive of penury as dire as I had supposed. I was shown into a drawing-room and there left for an appreciable interval to my own resources; this, too, carried an old-world effect; it is what happens regularly in Victorian novels. Then the door was briskly opened. It was a young woman who entered the room.

'Mr Siphon?'

'Syson.'

'Sorry. I know you're Robin's housemaster. I'm his sister, Julia. My mother isn't back yet, which isn't very polite. She's changing her book. Do sit down.'

I remembered that Robin's sister followed some secretarial occupation in the town. As it was barely eleven o'clock, I conjectured that this must be on a part-time basis. She was a good-looking young woman, and very like her brother. In temperament, I decided at once, she inclined to what I thought of as the 'hard' side of Robin's nature.

'She's always changing her book,' Julia said. 'She's taken to subscribing for only one at a time. She could have four at the public library for free. But she goes to one of those subscription places that are on their last legs anyway. The one book is simply an excuse for perpetually traipsing around. When she gets to the shop I believe she just grabs something at random. It's an excuse, as I say. For what Robin calls showing the flag.'

'Yes. He has called it that to me. It seems better than hiding a diminished head in shame: that sort of attitude.'

'There's a moderation in all things.'

After this exchange of platitudes, Julia and I looked at one another in silence. I had a feeling that she was trying to decide whether, although a schoolmaster, I was approximately human. Then she spoke again.

'Have you come to say Robin's back?'

'I'm afraid not.'

'Or that they've copped dad?'

'Not that either.'

'An open prison is a mouldy idea. Silly old man! I suppose he just couldn't help it. A prison should be all dungeons and iron bars and massively bolted doors. Then people wouldn't fret themselves over fatuous plans about how to get out. They'd just resign themselves to going through with it.'

I found nothing to say to these propositions, so we were silent again. I glanced round the room. It didn't suggest the exercise of much taste, or even interest. But the furniture included two or three very 'good' pieces—the sort of things, I thought, that come down to grandchildren through a younger son or daughter. If on one or the other side of the Hayes family there had been not too long ago persons of rank or consequence their present position would be all the more humiliating. But if this young woman felt like that, she didn't show it. She probably thought that I hadn't driven over to Uptoncester to much purpose. On the other hand, there was no suggestion in her manner that it hadn't been the natural thing to do. Her style of address was certainly a shade bald, but I felt I could get on with her. I didn't have that sort of confidence about her mother. In fact I hoped that Mrs Hayes would browse a little before grabbing that book.

'Is Robin,' I asked, 'by way of writing home regularly?'

'He writes to me. Mostly no more than would go on a postcard. But always in an envelope. Private.'

'There is a relationship of confidence between you?'

'Yes.' The sharpness with which Julia said this made my question appear cumbersome. 'That boy, for instance. The whole works.'

'David Daviot?'

'Of course.'

Yet again we were silent. I remembered how Robin had spoken to me about his sister, almost going out of his way to assert that it was with her mother that Julia was particularly close. But what Julia had just said surely contradicted this. I attempted to probe the discrepancy.

'Your mother isn't aware how often you hear from Robin?'

'Well, no—or not lately. He writes to me at the office. But of course he does a family letter from time to time. My mother would have been baffled, you see, by anything like this David Daviot thing. Outraged, I suppose, if she really took it in.'

'I see.' It was difficult to know how to proceed with this cool young woman. 'Robin has had to unburden himself, and it has been to you?'

'That's what I'm saying, isn't it? I didn't feel it to be

something going on wantonly behind my mother's back. But the generation gap comes in—particularly since our father's having had to be locked up.'

'I think I can understand that.' Although I said this, I believe I remained puzzled all the same. It was probably the first time I had heard the expression 'generation gap', although professional experience had made me aware of the thing itself. Even viewed from afar, there is often something distinctly rum about family life nowadays. 'And you haven't,' I asked, 'heard from Robin since this—this escapade began?'

'Not a word. And no family letter, either. We're both worried—the womenfolk left at home. A classical situation, no doubt.'

'Are you surprised, Miss Hayes, as well as worried?'

'Very. Silence. It's unlike him. Unaccountable.'

If these words startled me, it was because they almost echoed those of the last lady with whom I had discussed the vanished boy's behaviour.

'And money,' Julia Hayes added prosaically. 'He can't have much.'

'Well, no—it isn't so.' I hesitated for a moment. 'Your uncle gave Robin a great deal of money just before the thing happened. Put bluntly, an extravagant and scandalous amount of money. Your brother and his friend could live on it for months.'

'Uncle Jasper can be trusted to make mischief. The man's a shit.'

'I must admit I don't greatly care for him myself.' I tried not to show myself as shocked. Presumably I had never heard that honestly expressive word on a lady's lips before. In this interview I was learning all the time. 'But there it is,' I said. 'Robin with suddenly a great deal of money in his pocket, and with this David on his hands. What do you think he'd do?'

'Bring him straight here.'

'Really that?' Unquestionably I was astonished by what I had just heard—perhaps because it was so odd a variant, this time, upon Miss Sparrow's opinion: the same root idea, so to speak, but a different destination.

'Perhaps not *absolutely* straight. Robin would think—he's not incapable of thinking, you know—and then he would start to cool down. He'd bring David home, and then he'd try to open negotiations with that horrible old judge. Make him promise to remove his grandson from what he thinks of as that bestial School House.'

'But surely your mother would be puzzled at the boys' turning up?'

'She mightn't have been all that puzzled. There's that half-term *exeat*, isn't there? She might even see it as a kind of vengeful magnanimity—heaping coals of fire on the judge's head.'

It was at this moment that Mrs Hayes entered the room. She was as I remembered her: a full-breasted and tightly corseted woman who, although without anything (her hat excepted) old-fashioned about her dress, contrived to suggest something of the decorum of her class in a past age. A concession to the present one was a shopping basket out of which there protruded the corner of what was becoming known as a coffee-table book. I could understand thoughts about a generation gap coming into the head of any youthful person brought into contact with her. She must have cut a commanding figure on that magistrates' bench. Whether she had sat on it since her husband's professional lapse I didn't know. At the moment, if Owen Marchmont was to be believed (as he no doubt was), there were policemen keeping an unobtrusive watch on the lady's front door and others lurking in the back garden. From where I sat—or now stood upon the entry of my hostess—I could glimpse through the window the slender spire of Uptoncester Cathedral. I remembered Marchmont's more or less remarking, like Brack in *Hedda Gabler*, that people don't do such things—not within respectable ecclesiastical society. I even wondered whether the woman—not to speak of her daughter—was shadowed whenever she left the house, just in case she had contrived to arrange some tryst with her absconded spouse. There was really nothing to be said for Mr Hayes. The man was an unmitigated pest.

But I thought I was more entitled to this view than Mrs Hayes was. And Mrs Hayes had barely shaken hands with me—a gesture to which she contrived to lend an air of reluctant favour—before she was exuding the conviction that her husband was simply, so to speak, a bad mistake. Whether she thought Robin a bad mistake too didn't appear, since for the present at least she wasn't addressing her mind to his predicament.

'Everything has been done for him,' she said—and I realized that it was only as 'him' or 'he' that the head of the family would figure in her conversation. 'I employed my own knowledge of the circuit to retain a thoroughly reliable barrister. Not a Q.C. To have been obliged to have a junior counsel as well would have been injudiciously to inflate the thing, to say nothing of the expense. But a resourceful man. At the end of the affair he conjured up a very passable speech in mitigation out of pretty well nothing at all. And my own connections have been extremely forgiving—compassionate, it may be said. Only the day before his disappearing from Hutton Green, he was visited by my brother, Jasper Tandem. Jasper, living as he does in London, was able to take him down an extremely handsome bunch of grapes from Fortnum and Mason's. Mr Marchmont told me on the telephone that he hadn't even touched them. I asked that they should be given to the poor.'

During this extraordinary speech Julia Hayes had left the room. I thought she had perhaps been obliged to return to her office, but that more probably she found her mother in her present vein a little hard to take. This might well obtain even if between mother and daughter there was something of the close relationship Robin had suggested. After all, the two males of the family had united to create a state of affairs of a stiffly testing character. But meanwhile here I was alone with Mrs Hayes, and I had to find some manner of address to her.

'I am extremely sorry,' I said, 'that Mr Hayes's unconsidered action should give you so much distress. But you will understand that it is Robin who is chiefly in my own mind. I am very anxious that he should come back to Helmingham and settle down at least for the remainder of this term. Then, by the time that he goes up to Oxford, we can be fairly hopeful that the whole thing will have blown over and been forgotten.'

'It was he who insisted on sending Robin to Helmingham.' Mrs Hayes simply ignored the tenor of what (perhaps with no great conviction) I had said. 'I myself was strongly in favour of another public school, although at the moment I cannot remember quite which.' Mrs Hayes paused (and she didn't often pause) on this rather odd remark. 'It is clear,' she resumed, 'that Helmingham was a mistake. A bad school.'

I was scarcely able to believe my ears, and supposed the unhappy woman to be so distraught that she could actually forget for the moment to whom she was speaking.

'I deeply regret that you should have arrived at that conclusion,' I said as impassively as I could. 'But Mr Hayes entrusted your son to the school, and more particularly to my own care. I must do everything I can to help the boy out of his difficulties.'

'And School House in particular,' Mrs Hayes said. 'School House is very bad. And I suppose it is under the Head Master, which makes matters worse.'

'It is not. The housemaster is my colleague Mr Taplow. I am afraid I cannot usefully discuss School House with you, Mrs Hayes.'

'It is in School House that there has been this depraved boy called Daviot, whom my son has so foolishly attempted to—to redeem.'

'I have no evidence that David Daviot is depraved, madam. But, for one reason or another, there is no doubt that he has been unhappy, and that your son—it must be said impulsively and foolishly—has thought to rescue him.'

I suppose I was becoming more than a shade pompous. That 'madam' had been pompous without a doubt. But the woman was thoroughly provoking, and continued to be so.

'And Daviot,' she said, 'is a name I do not wish to hear. We know who this boy's grandfather is. And neither in his charge to the jury nor in his delivery of sentence did he mention *my* name.'

At this point it would not have been unreasonable in me to believe myself in a madhouse. There was no reason whatever why Mr Justice Daviot should have named Mrs Hayes, and good reason in common humanity for his not having done so. But the woman was actually contriving to feel that she had been slighted! It seemed to me that my visit to her had proved entirely abortive, and that the best that I could do was to take myself rapidly out of Uptoncester. But I recalled Marchmont's belief that I might pick up at least a little information which might help in tracing the missing solicitor—and I knew that the sooner he was run to earth the less likelihood was there of his further embroiling himself with the law. So I asked his wife a question.

'Have you any idea, Mrs Hayes, where your husband is most likely to be found? There seems no point in his remaining at large simply as a fugitive. It's not as if he were some spectacular criminal who might get away to Liberia or Brazil. Ten to one, he is probably undergoing a certain amount of useless discomfort at this very moment.' I designed this as what is called a 'forthright' speech, but was none too pleased with myself when I had uttered it. Mrs Hayes herself, however, seemed to judge it entirely in order.

'He is a very dangerous man,' she said with satisfaction. 'It has been my experience on the bench that thoroughly weak characters are often that. You wouldn't yourself, Mr Syson, expect a rather unsuccessful provincial solicitor to be vindictive before anything else. But *he* is. I have had a great deal to put up with, Mr Syson. A very great deal indeed. There is something quite irrational in it.'

Before this outburst, and for the moment, I could only be silent. Rather resentfully, I felt that there was indeed an element of the irrational almost everywhere I looked in this affair. But I was obliged to persevere with my inquiry, even if it involved adopting an almost bullying tone.

'Come, come, Mrs Hayes. Just where does this impression of your husband's character take us? What do you suppose him to be up to? Let us get that clear.'

'He's after him.'

This abrupt colloquialism, foreign to the speaker's usual style, was startling in itself. Considered in conjunction with what she had just said, it was even more so. I was being told that Mr Hayes had absconded from Hutton Green in order to avenge himself upon the man who had sent him there. And inevitably there at once came into my head what both John Stafford and I had concluded to be a persuasion equally bizarre in Sir Henry Daviot himself: that the Hayeses, father and son, had entered into a conspiracy to strike at him in some way through his innocent grandson—perhaps abetted in their wicked design by the objectionable Jasper Tandem.

I told myself at once that I didn't believe any of this—not for a moment. It was simply that when unaccountable events happened people all over the place took to having dotty ideas about them. But at the same time I found myself wishing I could remember more than I appeared able to do of that brief meeting with the convicted man in his prison. Had I come away from it with the slightest sense that I had been interviewing a potentially dangerous person? I was almost certain this wasn't so. But was it not true that my acquaintance with criminality of any sort didn't extend beyond the field of boys smoking in lavatories or slipping into a pub for a martini or a pint of beer? Mr Justice Daviot, who had spent much of his life gazing searchingly at suspected malefactors in the dock, was much less likely to be at sea in such matters than I was. But then again, it had at least been Stafford's impression that Daviot's suspicion had been something bobbing up in an inconsequent and eruptive fashion at odds with a customary more equable view of things.

Where, if anywhere, these speculations would have led me I don't know, for at this moment Julia Hayes came back into the room. She was carrying a couple of envelopes and a very small parcel or packet, presumably the product of a mid-morning postal delivery.

'Is Mr Syson staying to lunch?' she asked.

I suppose Julia may have required this information in order to make some domestic arrangement for which she was responsible. But it wasn't quite tactful, nor did her mother's reply much mend matters.

'Of course if that is what he finds convenient, Julia.'

I hastened, in what words I could command, to intimate that it was not, and a slight awkwardness ensued. Julia was considerate enough to think to relieve it by handing what she was carrying to her mother.

'A couple of bills, I expect,' she said. 'Let's hope they're not ghastly big ones, or shockingly overdue. I don't know about the parcel. It just says "Hayes", which seems a bit cavalier.'

Mrs Hayes might have been expected to defer inquiry into these matters until I had taken my leave and was out of the house. But—possibly prompted by the same financial anxiety as her daughter—she tore open one of the envelopes at once.

'That impertinent butcher!' she exclaimed, and opened the second. 'An appeal for the aged.' This she appeared to find impertinent too, since she crumpled the thing up and tossed it into a waste-paper basket. '"Hayes",' she read, as if she didn't much care for the name, and picked up the packet thus curtly addressed. 'Posted in London,' she added, in a tone suggesting that here was a circumstance distasteful in itself. 'If you will excuse me,' she said, with an unexpected excursion into civility. And she opened the packet.

What was revealed, rather casually wrapped in some tissue paper, was a wrist-watch on a broad expanding metal bracelet. It was the kind of watch, not then quite so common as now, which conveys a good deal more information than the mere time of day.

'How very absurd,' Mrs Hayes said. 'There must have been some mistake. "Hayes", you know. It suggests incompetence.'

'It's not absurd at all.' Julia spoke impatiently. 'That's Robin's watch. He must have sent it to be repaired at the end of the holidays, and been a bit brief with his name. Now it has just come back.'

'At least there isn't a bill with it.' Mrs Hayes had rummaged hastily to determine this, which was plainly the point of importance to her. She then dropped the watch into the drawer of a bureau, as if she took very little interest in it. No more did I, and I got up to take my leave.

At this Mrs Hayes promptly rang a bell to summon the

housemaid, who conducted me into the hall and handed me my hat. I wondered whether the poor girl, thus 'trained' to the rituals of a genteel household, was at all sure of her next month's wages.

# IX

I HAD TAKEN no pleasure in my visit to Robin's mother and sister, and was without the satisfaction of being able to feel that it had served a useful purpose. But now the scene in front of me was not at all disagreeable. Uptoncester asserted itself at once as a city inimical to sick hurry and divided aims: as consonant, in fact, with my own unashamedly conservative inclinations. In the quiet crescent in which the Hayeses' house stood commercial bustle didn't extend beyond a couple of messenger boys on bicycles with big baskets perched in front of the handlebars—just as they might have appeared on a picture postcard of the Edwardian era. Two clergymen had met in front of a pillar-box and were conversing with the tranquil cheerfulness of believing Christians. Two ladies exercised dogs—dogs as well trained, one felt, as Mrs Hayes's housemaid, justly claiming the modest freedom of lamp-posts but aware that they must not foul the footpath. Close to Mrs Hayes's well-swept front-door steps an unseasonable tourist (as he appeared to be) consulted what must have been a guidebook, rotating it as one does when trying to orientate oneself on a street-plan. The November noon was chilly but for the moment steeped in sunshine. Not far off, the cathedral bells chimed a quarter-hour.

I had been about to make my way to my car in the car park where I had left it, but now it came into my head to be a tourist too. My day was in a state of chronological muddle, since I had miscalculated the time that would be taken up by my mission, and my next engagement was to dine with Owen Marchmont at Hutton Green, a mere two hours' run from where I stood. I projected a visit to the cathedral, a sandwich and glass of beer in a pub, and then perhaps a further stroll, if the sunshine held, through the peaceful town and its environs.

The terrain was not very familiar to me, but at least I required no guidebook. Knowing where there was a tobacconist, I bought myself a couple of ounces of John Cotton 1 & 2. Locating a W.H. Smith, I acquired a newspaper to glance at over my lunch: this because everything was likely to close down for an hour at one o'clock. The west front of the cathedral was as pleasing as I remembered it: generously cluttered with statuary, some of it headless, as if in emulation of Exeter or Wells. I entered, and the interior held the solemn emptiness characterizing Anglican places of worship outside business hours. I wandered round for twenty minutes and there was only one other pilgrim: the man with the guidebook. We exchanged a few casual words. I did a further round—this time in the interest not of studying thirteenth-century architecture but of reading Latin epitaphs. Before one of these, of considerable elaboration, the man with the guidebook paused beside me again, and said 'Quite a lot they had to say about dad or mum, hadn't they?' I explained to him that in Greek an epitaph could be an entire funeral oration. He stared at me in amazement, and moved rather hastily away.

The early afternoon didn't hang heavily on my hands, since there is a good deal worth at least cursory inspection in Uptoncester. But eventually I found myself wandering quite far afield, and in consequence in contemplation of a very different scene. This was the industrial estate, which announced itself on a large but half-obliterated signpost pointing down a badly cracked and puddled asphalt road. I had driven past it on some previous occasion, so it didn't take me altogether unawares. And now, instead of turning back, I took it into my head to walk through it. I soon found that, as far as human frequentation went, I might as well have been in the central Sahara or the Nullarbor plain. Hastily built, I suppose, in anticipation of a boom that didn't come, its materials were for the most part no more permanent than breeze-blocks and galvanized iron. Perched above these low-hutched buildings were rusty tanks which had once provided a water supply, and trailing over them like the first tentative tendrils of a potentially obliterating vegetation were fallen electric cables which nobody had bothered to tidy up. Here and there stood more assuming mini-factories of discoloured brick; these had been lit by rows of windows projecting slant-wise from the roof, so that the effect was of some savagely toothed disarticulated lower jaw of a prehistoric monster. There wasn't an unbroken pane of glass in sight. I wondered whether this was the consequence of mere frost and gale and the effluxion of time, or whether there had been a period in which the less cultivated youth of Uptoncester had been in the habit of putting in happy holiday afternoons here with catapults and stones, so that the industrial estate had been for a time a ready-made 'adventure playground'.

All this tended to sombre reflection. I found a sheltered corner in which I could perch on an abandoned wooden crate in the scarcely warming sunshine, which still intermittently appeared through breaks in ominously leaden skies. I lit a pipe. (Schoolmasters were still allowed pipes in the 'seventies, although cigarettes were already taboo.) From the young proletarians who might have rampaged here my thoughts turned to my own sort of boy, and to what my own sort of school was trying to do for him. We were in a period, I told myself, in which the 'public' schools (for we were already prompted to use those self-conscious inverted commas) were returning to their traditional post-Arnoldian function in society. For a long time this had been largely in abeyance—in the sense that the majority of boys at these schools (Robin Hayes and Iain Macleod, for instance) had fathers who had been at similar schools before them. But now the comfortable squirarchy and the professional classes (but not the secure aristocracy) were being progressively priced out, so that once more we were largely coping with what used to be called 'new men', and had in fact the somewhat thankless role of introducing them to traditions and modes of feeling which year by year were becoming outmoded in the world at large. That motto from the sixth book of the *Iliad*—*AIEN APIΣTEYEIN*—was already substantially old-hat, unless by striving to excel was meant doing one's best to cut the other chap's throat in an increasingly desperate market-place.

These gloomy generalities were of a kind I didn't commonly

indulge myself in, and their cropping up puzzled me now. Partly, of course, the fit was occasioned by my dismal surroundings. But chiefly—I suddenly discovered—it represented a kind of masking of a much more specific anxiety. As these days had gone by, my fears about Robin Hayes had increased to an extent which, rather mysteriously, I found myself unwilling to acknowledge even to myself. It wouldn't be true to say that for his father I didn't care a bit. I did feel for the man and pity him. But his particular shipwreck was of a common enough sort, and a good whack of his life lay behind him. Moreover I had at least imagined myself to detect in him, not indeed the dangerousness in which his wife sought to discern a threat to the safety of Mr Justice Daviot, but rather a kind of impudent resilience hinting that he might surprise himself and others yet. But his son had his life before him, and there would be tragedy in his falling into folly which might hopelessly impede his career at its outset. Thus I explained to myself why I was anxious about Robin. And, of course, he was my top boy. Just for this term, for these two terms, he was in a unique relationship with me, distinct from my relationship with any other of my current boys.

Rather abruptly, I knocked out my pipe, stood up, and walked on. But I had got to the further edge of the area, and it occurred to me that if I continued ahead instead of turning back I should reach open country and be able to make my way to the city by a more agreeable circular route. I still had plenty of time for this.

What I came on almost at once was wholly unexpected. Instead of field and hedgerow and coppice, powdered with snow, I was confronted with a large expanse of sullen grey water: a roughly circular basin, artificial in suggestion, with a diameter of something like a quarter of a mile. If it was a reservoir, its water would need a good deal of purifying before it could issue from anybody's tap. But at once I knew I had seen such creations before. They have been vast gravel-pits, excavated to provide hard core for the fabricating of endless arterial roads, and left to fill up as Brobdingnagian puddles, unpopulated even by the humblest of fish. Perhaps a couple of minutes went by before I discerned that this one had, after all, been put to some use. There was a gate, and beside it, again, a half-obliterated sign. *Aquatic Leisure Park*, it said. *Sailing. Water Ski-ing. Schnorkels on hire. Try the fascinating new Planche à Voile.*

An aquatic park was surely a novelty in itself. But of course none of the activities solicited was at present taking place, since midwinter lay not far ahead. This, however, was not alone what was obvious. The aquatic park was as defunct as the industrial estate. A boat-house, a café, sundry gimcrack erections for subsidiary entertainment were mouldering and warping themselves away in a pervasive damp. Behind me, labour; ahead of me, play: neither had been a success. It added up, I told myself, to a society in decay. In the distance I could still see the cathedral spire, serenely beautiful. But the institution it symbolized wasn't doing too well either.

I turned round, to go back, after all, as I had come. As I did so, a figure moved in front of me, and then dodged rapidly into cover behind one of the nearer factory buildings. It was the man with the guide-book. I realized that I had been shadowed all day.

Owen Marchmont had as good as told me about it, after all: policemen on the doorstep and among the gooseberry-bushes. I could see the point of it. Any unidentified person visiting Mrs Hayes might be an accomplice of her husband's and bearing a message from him. Alternatively, he might be receiving from the lady directions as to a rendezvous in the unfrequented industrial estate or anywhere else. The plain-clothes officer trailing me had no doubt been discouraged as well as startled on receiving a scrap of information in the field of Greek etymology. But he had stuck to his job.

Was he sticking to it still? I asked myself this question as I drove out of Uptoncester. Logically, I surely remained a suspect until definitely identified, or exonerated by one means or another. But this degree of surveillance, if it extended to everybody happening in on the Hayeses, could not be other than a heavy tax on the resources of the police. As I realized this, a fresh notion occurred to me. Was it possible that Mrs Hayes was right, and that her husband was really 'after' Sir Henry Daviot? Was it possible, at least, that Sir Henry's own (as I judged them) dotty apprehensions as expressed in Tim Taplow's study were obliging the police to take quite exceptional measures? A judge of the High Court is, after all, a very important man.

Thus finding myself in a world of totally unfamiliar speculations, I began, I can now see, to turn a little dotty myself. I glanced continually at my driving-mirror, anxious to determine whether any identifiable vehicle was keeping unnaturally in contact with me. The idea of being followed by the police can turn itself very readily into the idea of being followed by criminals. I came near to seeing myself as that sort of hunted man, dear to novelists of low life and criminal practice, who has equally to fear pursuit by the lawless and the law. I might even have panicked, stepped on the accelerator and rammed myself into a tanker or a bus (that favourite climax of films and T.V. entertainments dealing in such nonsense) had not a sense of humour come to my aid. That I own a keen or ready sense of humour I would not aver. But I did find funny the fact that I was now making my way to a prison. My pursuer—if he existed—would feel uncommonly at a loss when I drew up before Hutton Green.

I drove faster than I would normally have done and continued to do so even when I had rationally assured myself that there was no frightful fiend behind me. The whole thing had, as the boys liked to say, 'shook' me. Had this not been so, I could scarcely have fallen into the extraordinary course of conduct which I was to embrace later that evening.

I had turned on my headlights in the dusk, and in no time it would be dark. Even so, I was going to arrive at Hutton Green awkwardly early. Marchmont had mentioned to me that some routine duty would be occupying him until shortly before seven o'clock, and that if I arrived before that I must simply 'make myself at home'. This troubled me. When I rang what had to be called his front-door bell it would presumably be answered by the same warder or 'screw' who had previously admitted me. It didn't appear possible to say, 'Is Mr Marchmont at home?' and

I suppose it would have to be something like, 'Good evening. I have a dinner engagement with the Governor'. Nothing could be less complicated, yet I found myself hesitating before the encounter. I seemed even in imagination to hear the jangling of a bunch of keys emanating from this anomalous portal-guarding person.

In this absurd frame of mind I drove into Hutton Green very shortly after six o'clock, and as I once more sought—this time in pitch darkness—the drive-way to the prison, what I first became aware of was an illuminated sign comprising a species of heraldic shield and the words *Hutton Arms Hotel*. I recalled this as a hostelry of an evidently superior sort, which had probably once provided good entertainment for man and beast, and in this later age did a certain amount of residential business in a weekending way. I found myself drawing up before it. To put in half an hour here would solve my chronological problem. And I felt like a drink.

There was a lounge of modest size, with a big open fire, and there was only one guest on view. Or partially on view, since he was sitting on one side of the fire-place behind an open copy of *The Times*, and thus exhibited nothing but a pair of well-polished shoes and equally well-tailored lower limbs. I rang a bell and was brought my drink with commendable speed almost as soon as I had settled down to warm myself on the other side of the fire. I was now alone with the stranger, and he lowered his newspaper in order to take civil account of me.

'An inclement evening,' he said, 'but with some pleasant sunshine earlier in the day.' I concurred in this view. 'Mr Syson, is it not?' the stranger added with mild interest. And I realized that I was in the presence of Robin Hayes's father.

It was a considerable shock, and some interest must attach to the fact that I immediately accounted for Mr Hayes's appearance in an ingeniously reasonable way. Owen Marchmont, who was clearly a much occupied man, had been under some misapprehension as to the circumstances in which Mr Hayes had departed from his establishment. Mr Hayes was simply on parole, and had put up in the nearest agreeable lodging. I had even said feebly, 'I'm glad to see you', before acknowledging to myself that this was *not* a reasonable idea at all. And Mr Hayes was amused.

'Did you ever,' he asked, 'read a story by Edgar Allan Poe called "The Purloined Letter"?'

'Yes.'

'It turns upon the invisibility of the glaringly obvious. If one were inclined to take a little break from that amiable Harrovian's set-up over the way, where would it be most natural to go? Obviously to the nearest comfortable pub.' Mr Hayes chuckled. 'I don't doubt that they're hunting for me, you know, through the length and breadth of the land. But it hasn't occurred to them to look in here. The cuisine isn't half bad.'

I was silent for a moment, recalling my sense that there was some odd potentiality hidden in this petty embezzler. But I didn't know what to do, and took refuge in a wholly inappropriate lightness of tone.

'I'm glad to hear it,' I said. 'But don't you find it comes a shade expensive?'

'Ah, you forget my brother-in-law. I believe you've met him. Jasper Tandem. Do you know, I've never succeeded in touching him for more than a penny or two before? But he came down handsomely with quite a wodge of the stuff.'

'Under a bunch of grapes?'

'Just that.' Mr Hayes seemed slightly surprised. 'And with various other convenient dispositions as well.'

'I see.'

In fact I believed myself to see quite a lot. Tandem's conduct towards his brother-in-law almost duplicated his conduct towards his nephew. In both instances there had been a big hand-out of money in the interest of pure mischief of a more or less malign order. Tandem's character was that of the Vice in the Old Play. It wasn't to be supposed that he at all cared for Mr Hayes (or for Robin either). Uncomfortable consequences for the escaped man were almost bound eventually to attend his freakish escapade. But at least one reassuring fact seemed to me to be evident. Mr Hayes had certainly not left Hutton Green in order to prosecute some hideous vengeance against Sir Henry Daviot and his grandson. So Robin's departure from

Helmingham, even if in some way connected with his father's behaviour, was equally innocent so far as anything of the kind was concerned. Of course I had known this. The notion that Robin had carried off David as part of a hideous conspiracy could not have any existence outside the mind of that aged judge in one of his unnervingly unbalanced moments. And now Mr Hayes's relaxed holiday attitude made this so clear that for a moment I felt a positive affection for the man.

'I'm afraid,' I said, 'there isn't particularly good news of Robin. I don't know whether you've heard.'

'At the moment, Mr Syson, as you can imagine, I don't hear much not judged worthy of record in newspapers of the more sober sort.' Mr Hayes tapped *The Times*. 'Is the boy in trouble again?'

'I'm not aware that he has been in anything that could be called trouble before. What has happened now is simply that he has left Helmingham in a somewhat irregular fashion.'

'I'm delighted to hear it—irregular or not. As his affairs now stand—Oxford, and so on—he's only wasting money and time. Has he got himself a job?'

'I can't say as to that, but I think it improbable. He has left me, taking with him a younger boy from another house.' I paused on this. 'A boy called Daviot.'

'Dear me! I know the name.'

'Quite so.'

'And Daviot is rather old, surely, to have a son in his early teens. If it's a son of the judge that you're talking about.'

'David Daviot is the judge's grandson. Where the two boys have made off to, we don't know. But their departure followed immediately upon its becoming known at Helmingham that you have—well, taken the course you are now embarked upon. And I think it fair to tell you that the coincidence has put some disturbing ideas in Sir Henry Daviot's head.'

'It wouldn't take much to do that.'

I was silent for a moment following this brisk comment, and wondered whether there was much point in going on. If Mr Hayes were at all interested in his son's untoward conduct, he gave no sign of it. But then I did continue.

135

'Mr Hayes, would you describe yourself as feeling any particular animosity towards Sir Henry?'

'Good lord, no! The old boy was very decent about the whole thing.'

'You didn't—well, shall I say cause any kind of disturbance at the conclusion of that trial? Threaten the judge from the dock—that kind of thing.'

'My dear man! You must be aware that I am an Officer of the High Court. Is it likely that I should behave in a disrespectful manner?' Mr Hayes came out with this quite magnificently, so that I positively felt rebuked. I changed the subject abruptly.

'May I ask,' I said, 'what are your further plans? I'd imagine that after a time even the good cuisine of the Hutton Arms would pall.'

'Oh, as to that, I shall simply clock in again over the way.' Mr Hayes thus expressed his intention with perfect ease. 'There will be a certain awkwardness, no doubt. They'll be disappointed in me, you know. That kind of thing. On the other hand, turning up again will be a considerable virtue in me. And they won't want too much fuss. They'd look so ridiculous—wouldn't they?—if my little Hutton Arms ploy got into the papers.' As this thought came to Mr Hayes he waved his copy of *The Times* gracefully in air.

I rose to take my leave. Would Mr Hayes go upstairs to change for dinner—into a dinner-jacket, a dark suit? That he was enjoying himself, that his freedom was fun, I didn't doubt. Unconcern was his key-note—and not least over whatever occasion had brought me to Hutton Green.

I found myself shaking hands with Mr Hayes. It is an action that ought never to be of a totally faithless order. So what on earth was I to do? I was still pondering this question as I drove away from the hotel.

## X

'Visitors,' Owen Marchmont said, '—and outstaying their welcome, bless them. Visitors in a technical sense, that is. A Board of them. They inquire into things, you know, and are invariably gratified by how the place is going.' Marchmont was already pouring me a drink as he spoke. 'Thank God, no need for another word of shop tonight.'

It was a crucial moment. I ought to have said at once, 'I'm afraid one piece of shop there is—and it's rather urgent'. But I didn't. If anybody apart from myself was to blame for my silence, it was the author of a play I had seen as a boy. Perhaps it was by John Galsworthy—a writer now, I believe, not particularly well thought of. I don't really remember. What I do seem to remember is that there is a judge in it. He is on a fishing holiday, or possibly he is shooting things. He must be on fairly unfrequented territory, since he is able to hold a long colloquy with an escaped convict. There they are together, you see, but it's man to man and no longer judge and the prisoner he had sentenced. How the situation was resolved is another thing I don't recall, although clearly in my head is the expensive tea-shop my aunt took me to after the matinée. I now wonder whether in the course of the action the judge unwarily shook hands with the fugitive. It seems unlikely. Of course I didn't reflect on all this as I stood in Marchmont's comfortable living-room. It was only some years afterwards that the analogy bobbed up in my mind. At the moment I was much too busy with the raw fact of my predicament.

That it was a genuine predicament, I confidently assert. There we were, two Harrovians of what wits like to call the old school, with the thing between us. Marchmont must have noticed something ill at ease about me, but only as behaviour he was accustomed to. A prison is an odd place in which to be asked out to dinner.

Perhaps I told myself that, so far as I knew, Mr Hayes's crime had occasioned no specific hurt to any individual. It had been what they call a crime against society. Of course this line of thought doesn't really stand up. Robin had been hurt, and so had those two women in Uptoncester. But if this thought came to me, it was without effect. I just couldn't—couldn't for the moment—give the man away. I couldn't sneak on him. Yet this meant that I was now my schoolfellow's guest on false pretences. I was abusing his hospitality.

Feebly, I assured myself that there was plenty of time. Mr Hayes was at his ease in the Hutton Arms. My turning up on him hadn't alarmed him in the least, and it was his intention to come back to Hutton Green of his own volition when his little 'ploy' ceased to entertain him. I expose myself here to a charge of singularly naïve thinking. But so it was.

We talked, as we began our meal, on wholly indifferent matters. But Marchmont's conception of 'shop' didn't extend to the entire Hayes affair, and he asked me about Robin and the young David. I told him we were still in the dark, and then gave him some account of my visit to the ladies of the Hayes family. I added—with some attempt to be amusing—the information that in Uptoncester I had been doggedly shadowed by the police. Marchmont received this with a suitable brisk laugh, but at the same time I saw that he was sceptical about it. This annoyed me (as may be imagined, I was in considerable disarray) and when Marchmont became aware of this he changed the subject at once. We went back to talk about past times, and the evening thus wore away. An observer uninformed about my situation would have judged that here simply was one of those reunions that don't quite come off. I was unhappy about this, for in fact I had come to like Owen Marchmont.

I was already thinking that by pleading the drive ahead of me I could soon decently take my leave, when he made an abrupt plunge into shop, after all.

'Pog, have you heard that this old devil Daviot has been creating?'

'Creating, Owen?' This use of the word was new to me.

'Making the deuce of a racket over the fuzz failing to pick up my unfortunate Father Hayes. A harmless old nuisance, as I think we are agreed.'

'Yes, indeed,' I said—I suspect with idiotic eagerness.

'But old Daviot doesn't see it like that. I gather from a chap in the Home Office that he has actually been badgering the Minister. He is convinced that Hayes *père* and Hayes *fils* are in a conspiracy against him—and are even proposing to use Daviot *petit-fils* as instruments of their vengeance.'

'Totally absurd.'

'Yes, of course. Yet—in a way—I wonder.'

'Wonder what about, Owen?'

'About just what is going on.' Marchmont looked at me in detectable perplexity as he confessed to this vagueness. 'Where the devil are those two kids? Old Hayes, you know, has a streak of the flamboyant to him. I'd not be surprised if he proved to be up to something entirely odd. Would you agree, Pog?'

'Well, yes.' It wasn't possible for me to say less than this.

'You'll know better than I do whether that goes for his boy as well. But at least he has made a large gesture in bolting with that particular man's grandson. So I'd expect him to contrive a further gesture or two as he goes along. But nothing. Silence.'

This unnerved me—usefully, indeed, since it alerted me, well within the hour, to what was at the moment no more than an obscure circumstance tucked away in my mind. I can come to the occasion at once.

My good-bye was contrived, I hope, in decent form, and I set off for Helmingham. It was pitch dark and very cold. I always drive cautiously after dining out, and now my caution was increased by apprehensions of black ice on the roads. Even so, my thought wandered at times. It flitted over this and that in the whole ghastly affair. Chiefly, for a start, I continued to chew over that evening's luckless issue. As a law-abiding member of the public I had behaved most improperly. I ought to have told Marchmont about Mr Hayes the moment I came into his presence. Indeed, instantly upon recognizing the escaped man I ought, no doubt, to have endeavoured to effect a citizen's arrest. That, I believe, is the term. Instead of which I had obeyed some entirely dubious private code which probably had a good dash of cowardice, moral cowardice, to it. And it was all dreadfully mixed up with my feelings about Robin Hayes. I had protected his father out of an utterly muddled notion that I was thereby protecting him.

So then I thought about the whole course of my handling of Robin in his peculiar family predicament. I went over my encounters with him. I came to the last but one of them.

I have already hinted that this was a memory intensely painful to me, more painful even than his subsequently addressing me with incredible words. It was the moment of his flipping his uncle's disgraceful cheque pretty well in my face. As if vividly through the darkness in front of my windscreen, I saw this again now. I *saw* it. It was there almost with the quality of a hallucination. I saw the cheque. I saw the hand holding it. *And I saw a wrist-watch as well.*

It was the same wrist-watch that had arrived by post in Uptoncester. Unless my memory was playing tricks with me (which was possible, although I didn't believe it) this was the fact of the matter. I started counting days, but really I scarcely needed to do so. That there had been time to send the watch to be repaired (even if, preoccupied as he was, Robin had thought of that) and for it to have arrived back in Uptoncester as it had done, was on the face of it implausible. So here was a small mystery. Or, rather, here was nothing of the sort. Here was a mystery evoking a sense of menace in what I had no means of seeing as other than a totally unaccountable way. I was rather frightened. Without arriving, even in imagination, at any specific context in which to place the thing, I was exactly that. And then I saw one consequence with clarity. Anything I knew about any Hayes, the police ought to know.

I was running through a village as this came to me, and into my headlights there swam a telephone kiosk in a providential fashion. I braked hard, and was inside it within seconds. Within further seconds Hutton Green was answering me, and I was put through to Marchmont straight away. He was recruiting himself with a final whisky, I imagine, after rather a boring evening.

'Owen? It's Robert.'

'Robert?'

'Syson. Pog, if you like. It's about Hayes. He's in the Hutton Arms.'

'The Hutton Arms! Is this a joke?'

'Nothing of the sort. I went in for a drink.' This was dreadfully embarrassing in itself. 'You see, I was a little too early for you.'

'Go on.'

'And there he was—as a resident guest. I somehow couldn't bring myself to tell you.'

'Hold the line.'

I held the line, and thought I heard a call being made on another telephone. I had to put more money into the machine. Then Marchmont spoke again.

'I've sent across my own chaps,' he said. 'Stretching things a little, but there's the point that it's quicker than contacting the local police. Time seems an element.'

'He said he intends to stay on for a short time longer, and then clock in with you again.'

'Did he, indeed. Now, Pog, listen. You went into that pub, and there was this chap. He was in a poor light, or reading a paper or something, so you really had no more than a glimpse. He seemed hauntingly familiar, but you didn't think much about it. Then, as you were driving back to Helmingham, it suddenly came to you. So you got on this blower at once. Got that?'

'Yes. But we had quite a talk. He'll divulge that.'

'Not after I've negotiated with him, he won't. So now go home and sleep soundly. The impudence of the man! Rather jolly, really.'

'But, Owen, there's another thing. There's the wrist-watch.'

'The what?'

'The wrist-watch. Robin's.'

This produced a short silence. It must have been coming to Marchmont that I was distraught.

'Ah, the wrist-watch,' he said. 'Is it important?'

'I think so, but I can't imagine why. It came by post in rather an odd way while I was with those women in Uptoncester. They opened the little parcel and there it was: Robin's watch.'

'Come back.'

'What?'

'Pog, please turn round and come back to Hutton Green now. I can put you up for the night. After we've had a chat about that watch, of course. You have the inside of a week still clear of the school, haven't you?'

'Yes—more or less.'

'Then that's fine. I'll expect you. But don't hurry too much. The roads may be turning not too good. Remember the wise Onslows. *Festina lente.*'

With this not very learned joke, Owen Marchmont rang off.

As it happened, there was more *lente* to it than *festina*. I turned the car round—at least I was capable of that—and then promptly, in what was becoming a damnably threatening November night, I got lost.

It was partly because the roads abruptly turned treacherous. Once or twice the car glided beneath me in disconcerting directions. The effect was that my mind became concentrated all the time on the next hundred yards. If there were sign-posts, I didn't notice them. Actually my car was equipped with what I took some pride in as a very cunning device: a spot-light high up on a corner of the windscreen that could be swung on an arc by manipulating a knob conveniently to hand in the interior. I can recall the salesman making much of it in his showroom among all the marvellous things I was going to get for my money. I didn't remember to use this mini-searchlight now. In no time, just as if I was piloting a yacht or an aeroplane, I found myself hopefully studying the stars. The absurdity of this, when I realized it, produced the same sort of panic that can be occasioned by a sudden mechanical breakdown. One knows perfectly well that—after some inconvenience, no doubt—there is a drink and a bed securely in front of one. But the sudden powerlessness, literally that, renders one a poltroon for the nonce.

Naturally I got on top of this fairly quickly. But I had another impediment to contend with: an obsessively wandering mind. When I ought to have been considering the next fork before me, I was thinking about my recent bad conduct, or about Robin's watch. About this latter anxiety there was almost something precognitive. In an obscure sense, I was prepared.

When at length I reached Hutton Green, it was past one o'clock in the morning, and freezing fast. It was reasonable to suppose that Marchmont would have given me up. The place was in darkness. It wasn't the sort of prison in which electricity blazes down on a perimeter all night. The inmates, I told myself sardonically, had long since had their nice cup of something to ward off nocturnal starvation, and were tucked up beneath their eiderdowns. Such a fantasy wasn't amusing. I was ashamed of it. I rang a bell.

The door was opened by a turnkey (an expressive word, which appears to have fallen into disuse) not previously known to me. He was probably one of those whose employment was to prowl the place at night, occasionally peering through little shuttered spy-holes at slumbering men. This was a dismal thought, and he was dismal himself—and I felt, moreover, that there was something sinister in the glance he cast on me. All Hutton Green, or all of it that was not sound asleep, probably knew by this time how badly the Governor's guest had behaved. Or so I was convinced. A minute later I was further discomfited by discovering that Marchmont was no longer alone and no longer in his pleasant living-room. He was back in his office, and his companion was introduced to me as Mr Ogilvy, a Deputy Assistant Commissioner of Metropolitan Police. A Deputy Assistant anything sounded to me initially as pretty small beer, but then I reflected that a Commissioner is somebody so exalted that this was probably not so. And Mr Ogilvy seemed to feel that it would be courteous to explain himself.

'I've been apologizing to Marchmont,' he said, 'for barging in—and uncommonly rapidly at that. On invitation, of course.'

I gave this a nod, judging it to be a matter of punctilio on which comment was not required.

'Of course Sir Henry Daviot lives within our District,' he went on, 'and that's a factor in the thing. But there's also the nature of what seems to be happening. It's only three years ago that we had the first ever recorded instance of it in England. A clumsy amateur affair, and the villains are in prison now. But—as you no doubt recall, Mr Syson—the victim on that occasion died.' ('Three years' before the events I am describing means, of course, something more than a decade ago, since I am looking back on and recording these from my position as a retired man.)

I stared blankly at Ogilvy, having no idea what he was talking about. It was only clear to me that he was out to alarm. Marchmont, quite aware of this, felt that he must put in a word.

'You'll understand, Robert, that I've had to tell Mr Ogilvy about what happened at the Hutton Arms a few hours ago. He has brought me news making it quite essential that all cards should be put on the table, so to speak. But at least we can be orderly about it. And the first fact is simply this: Hayes lost no time in clearing out of that pub. He wasn't being quite honest, I'm afraid, when he suggested to you that he had a sense of comfortable leisure before him.'

At least I wasn't so guileless as not to have expected this.

'Oh, dear!' I said. 'I'm frightfully sorry.'

There was a moment's silence, and the helplessness of my reaction appeared to exercise a mollifying effect upon the Deputy Assistant Commissioner, so that I wondered—inconsequently—whether here was another Harrovian.

'It's regrettable, Mr Syson, I'm bound to say. But of course you could have no notion of the gravity of the issues involved. I do understand the thing. Speaking on a purely personal level, I'd like to say that. But, you see, so far as Hayes is concerned, we just don't know where we are. What was he up to from that extremely ingenious hiding-place? We have to face it. He may have been master-minding the whole thing.'

I began to think that I was hearing the word 'thing' rather too often.

'If I'm to be told of a very grave happening,' I said with some return of spirit, 'I'd like it to be now. But I have myself something to say at once. The idea of this man Hayes master-minding anything seems extremely far-fetched to me. I know that Sir Henry Daviot has something of the sort in his head. He believes—or at times he believes—that Hayes and Hayes's son are fabricating some vengeful conspiracy against him. When he is asserting anything of the kind, it's possible to judge him not quite right in the head.'

'Quite so, Mr Syson, quite so. Between ourselves, that is, quite so.' Ogilvy was unperturbed by the injudicious vehemence of what I had said. 'Only, you know, everything at the moment can be seen two ways on. Take Hayes's son, who I understand to be your pupil. And take his wrist-watch.'

'His wrist-watch!' I exclaimed—I believe in some dismay.

'Of course I've told Ogilvy about that,' Marchmont struck in. 'And, Robert, there's something I'd like to ask you about it. When those two women opened the packet and found it, were they frightened in any degree?'

'I don't think so. Puzzled, and looking for some explanation. But not frightened.'

'What about yourself?'

'I thought very little about it. At first, that is. But somehow it has come back to me since in what I can only call an obscurely sinister way. A kind of growing worry.'

'Exactly!' Ogilvy said—and in a tone of satisfaction I didn't care for. 'The cleverness lies there. And it has the interest of something new to me. It hasn't been uncommon on the continent and in America. But I imagine there has been only a handful of cases over here. But, Mr Syson, please consider this. Your pupil may be a free agent—but in a sense his father's agent—pretending to be in a very different situation. It's the implication of that state of affairs that you judge to be highly implausible. Alternatively, your pupil may actually be in that same situation. Is the wrist-watch—taken along with something to which I shall presently come—a kind of bluff? We have to ask ourselves that.'

'We also have to ask ourselves,' Marchmont said, 'whether what has now so upset Sir Henry is what it claims to be, or is a hoax, or is a kind of impromptu cashing-in on the part of some casual crook.'

When I say that I remained completely bewildered by all this,

I shall certainly strike the reader as decidedly slow in the uptake. The impression is again a matter of that decade. My companions, who might both be described as professional criminologists, were themselves pioneering novel ground. But at least I wasn't to remain groping much longer. Ogilvy, I judge, *wanted* to bewilder me. He had probably been by no means assured that I was not, in some obscure fashion, a villain myself. In a sense, he was trying me out. But now he had made up his mind about that, and when I exclaimed with mounting irritation, 'What the devil are the two of you talking about?' he answered briskly and with a single word.

'Kidnapping.'

'Kidnapping?' I could only repeat the word. It merely suggested to me, in the first place, a romance by Robert Louis Stevenson; and, in the second, what a dictionary tells one about the origin of the term as an act of carrying off by force a person or persons likely to be useful in a servile station.

'Kidnapping, or a pretence of it,' Marchmont amplified helpfully.

'Seizing and holding to ransom.' Ogilvy was being more helpful still. 'You might call it a modern variant of a habit well-established among the knightly classes in medieval times. And now I'll tell you, Mr Syson, just why I'm here at Hutton Green. It's the last known address, so to speak, of this man Hayes. And I'm demonstrating to Sir Henry Daviot how quick we are to leave no stone unturned. I've conferred with the local police—and now here I am, at this unholy hour, conferring with Marchmont. And, as it happens, with yourself. Whether it's a useful exercise remains to be seen. Daviot, who is an old man although still a formidable one, has had the hell of a shock—and one that might appear to vindicate some of those notions that have been wandering through his head. We must show him, as I say, that we are doing everything we possibly can.'

I believe I saw at once one way in which this was being done. A Deputy Assistant Commissioner would not normally be the person to go chasing round in such a situation. One would have expected an officer styled 'Detective Superintendent' or the like to be engaged in this bloodhound exercise. Once more it was necessary to recall that a Judge of the High Court is a very important man.

'Just what has been the shock?' I asked. For what the point is worth, I was ceasing to be fussed, and my mind was now working clearly enough.

'Round about the time of that parcel's being delivered to the ladies in Uptoncester, Sir Henry received a telephone call. And what was said to him, he wrote down at once. That sort of ability comes, I suppose, of long sitting on the bench.' Ogilvy produced this on a note of some admiration, and I have no doubt he was right. 'What he heard was this: "We've got those two boys, Daviot, and if you want them back alive, our conditions must be met. You'll be hearing from us again when we think fit". And at that the caller rang off.'

'Marchmont said something about a hoax,' I said. I had to say something, although anything adequate in face of this staggering information was utterly beyond me.

'Well, yes. I don't suppose that two boys decamping from your school has exactly made national news. But I do suppose that it has got around a little, their names included. So anybody with a grudge against the judge—or perhaps merely looking idly around for a joke—may have made that telephone call to him.'

'That kind of thing happens?'

'Certainly it does. There are nutters who regularly look out for people revealed as in some distress, and who then get on the telephone to them. But not often, I think, to this sort of effect. Usually it's just obscenities.'

'And Marchmont also said something about a casual crook cashing in.'

'You can see the idea there. Swift enterprise. Your villain hears of a presumably well-heeled old gent in anxiety about the disappearance of a child. The villain knows nothing about it. But he reckons he can conceivably shock a quick hand-out from the old chap by talking in a blood-curdling way.'

'But I've never heard of it actually happening,' Marchmont thought to interject. 'It's just a notion.'

'Surely,' I said, 'both these notions are knocked out of court by the wrist-watch?'

147

'Exactly.' Ogilvy was good enough to nod approval. 'And meant to be. Theoretically, it's conceivable that the boy sent the watch willingly to his mother and sister. That he is, in fact, part of a plot. Sir Henry could possibly manage to believe that, so we must show him it's in our heads. I can't say it's honestly in mine. And as for you, Mr Syson, I almost feel I have to apologize to you for mentioning it.'

'Not at all.' I can't think how dully I said this. 'It's your job to test out everything. But suppose we agree on the probability that a criminal abduction has taken place, and with the intention of extorting money by menaces. What happens next?'

'Perhaps nothing for quite some time. It was like that in the 1969 affair. Several longish silences. It's my view that they were occasioned by mere incompetence. The villains, as I mentioned, were amateurs, and found themselves puzzled about how to go ahead. But it certainly increased tension. And in other parts of the world, where this kind of thing has been happening quite a bit, long silences have been deployed precisely with that aim in view.'

For some time we were ourselves silent after this. I needn't expatiate on how I myself felt. It was all rather new to me. I'd led a sheltered life.

'Of course,' Marchmont was pursuing easily, 'it must be occurring to you that they could well have had a shot at nobbling this David on an earlier occasion. If they held their hand, it was perhaps from a feeling that coincidence was bringing such a lot their way. We needn't regard them as *intelligent*, you see. Outside the story-books, villains very seldom are. Their common card is *cunning*—which has its limitations, praise the Lord. It sometimes leads to complex capers when something much simpler would be the effective thing. You get what I mean?'

'Yes, indeed,' I said—perhaps not with great conviction.

'And there's another point about them. They're patchy. One moment you feel up against something wholly formidable, and the next you've come on a soft spot that smashes them. It's partly, no doubt, that the beggars'—and here Marchmont favoured me with a brief ironic glance—'probably haven't enjoyed much of the benefits of education.'

'No Double Firsts,' I said, rather feebly.

'Definitely not. But to come back to the cunning. It may well be that the calculating brand of silence is in operation, and that there will be more of it. Although first—do you know?—I'd rather expect a stepping-up of the wrist-watch effect.'

## XI

DRIVING BACK TO Helmingham next morning, I felt like a man who has left behind him in a railway carriage a half-finished detective story. The puzzle remained, but I was deprived of the means of pursuing it. Any effort of my own would be entirely amateurish, and the two professionals with whom it had pleased the Deputy Assistant Commissioner to say I had been 'conferring' were going their own way about the matter. Moreover I hadn't been as useful as I might have been. There was at least one point I ought to have made that I had forgotten all about. Not long before the disappearance of the boys, a suspicious character or characters had been in contact with David Daviot. There was the incident in an unfrequented part of the school grounds reported to me by Father Edwards, and there had been David's own story of an approach made to him in a public park. The notion of an authentic talent-scout from the theatrical world was absurd, but a crook nosing around to spy out the boy's habits and ideas and particular friendships was another matter. I ought to have reported on that.

There was something else that, so far as I could remember, we hadn't touched upon. Sir Henry Daviot was an eminent person, at least in a conventional sense of the term. His judgements would often be in print; his birthday would be recorded in newspapers; that kind of thing. But was he a man of any wealth? Criminals setting up in this comparatively new field of kidnapping for profit had the pick of all England to choose from. Robin Hayes, the son of a small embezzler, would make no appeal to them at all, and it was presumably only his being David's companion at a critical moment that had been the occasion of his abduction. But how much more attractive a prize was the judge's grandson? Judges were not at that time (nor are they, I believe, now) strikingly well paid. As barristers they might still have accumulated a small private fortune before being elevated to the bench. But unless they were also men of inherited wealth they would scarcely be prime targets for well-informed criminals.

This last thought was a particularly disturbing one, and it led me to a reconsideration of what I had been inclined to dismiss as a fantastic persuasion on Sir Henry's part. Perhaps, after all, revenge and not cupidity was the mainspring of the affair. The telephone message the judge had received appeared not quite to square with this—unless, indeed, a thirst for vengeance was to be assuaged by a kind of fine. But it remained a nasty possibility.

As I drove into the school grounds, with their round dozen of big bleak brick houses scattered irregularly round the perimeters of cricket fields and rugger grounds, their newer utilitarian blocks of class-rooms and labs, their centre in the incongruous Gothic chapel heaved up like a stranded whale, I became conscious of the emptiness of the place. There were no boys. There were no boys either hurrying and shouting and (a Helmingham phrase) ballyragging around, or sedately walking with an open book in the hope of rapidly making up on prep undone. The boys had all gone away, but would return on Sunday evening—all except David Daviot and Robin Hayes. I seem to recall that it was the alien character of what had happened, its remoteness from normal Helmingham life, that held my mind, overshadowing even the horrific threat implicit in the situation.

It had begun to snow, so heavily that during the last few miles of my run everything had been turning white as I drove. Within inches of the snug interior of the car I knew that on every side there lurked piercing cold. In Heynoe, until I turned up the central heating, it would be none too warm. My housekeeper was absent, and the two middle-aged women who formed its remaining resident staff had quarters of their own, adequately heated, in a remote corner of the building. I reflected glumly that I possessed no house, no home, in my own right. Heynoe was merely a hypertrophied tied-cottage. When the place had done with me as a housemaster I'd simply be out on my ear. It was as I drew up before the front door (the door upon which Robin had inflicted such damage) that the self-indulgent character of these musings shocked me, and I was overwhelmed by a new and dreadful question. Just what did this sudden, savage, premature winter—for it was now that—mean to the captive boys? In what sort of conditions might they be held by men who could make to Sir Henry Daviot such a telephone call as he had received? I was back with the monstrous unexpectedness of what had entered my life. It was as if I had gone to sleep securely here at Helmingham and woken up in the Chicago of Al Capone.

I suppose I was in a confused state of mind. I got out of the car and opened the boot to take out a suitcase which wasn't there; I had forgotten that my night's absence had been unpremeditated. I put the car away, took off my overcoat, picked up some letters from the hall table, and set about finding myself something to eat. Before I got far with this there was a ring at the front-door bell, and on returning to the hall I saw through a window a car very much grander than my own, together with some indication of a male person standing on the doorstep. I decided—I don't know why—that here was that sort of pestilential prospective parent who turns up without notice at an inconvenient hour and expects to be shown round the entire school. But business is business, and at Heynoe it was comfortable regularly to have a longer waiting-list than I might be able to accept. So I opened the door prepared to be adequately welcoming. It was to find myself confronted by Jasper Tandem.

There was nobody in England whom, at that moment, I less wanted to see. This man's freakish folly—or worse—had surely been at the root of the entire calamity confronting us. He had money—clearly he had no end of money—and he had scattered a lot of it in the interest of what was certainly meant to be mischief and had in fact been disaster. He had given his nephew a thousand pounds and thus encouraged him to behaviour resulting, however obscurely, in hideous misadventure—and had further thrown the boy off balance, I didn't doubt, by having already provided Mr Hayes with the means to effect his foolish escape from Hutton Green.

Whether these censorious thoughts were going through my head as I recognized Tandem on my doorstep I don't know. Quite probably not. I was certainly telling myself that there would be no point in preaching at the man.

'Ah, Syson!' he said—apparently in surprise that I should myself have to answer my doorbell. 'I hope this is a convenient time for a call?'

I looked at my watch (which wasn't exactly polished behaviour) and saw that it was a quarter to one. There was no escaping the implication of this.

'Not at all,' I said (thoroughly weakly). 'You won't have lunched? I'm alone, and was just about to find myself something. Will you join me?'

Predictably, Tandem said that he would, and I went through the proper rituals of taking his coat, asking him if he'd care to wash after his drive, finding him a glass of sherry, and then going in search of a meal that turned out to be chiefly a cold ham. What was thus created was a first-class false situation. Once the man had a knife and fork in his hands I was obliged to see the thing civilly through.

'A bad situation, this,' Robin's uncle said comfortably—or rather, perhaps, with an affectation of that, since I felt that actually he was in a condition of considerable alarm. 'My brother-in-law, for a start. I can't imagine what has prompted him to such folly. I visited him, my dear Syson, only the day before he bolted, and at least he didn't seem wrong in his head.'

I believe I resented 'My dear Syson' even more than the impudence of the whole statement. He couldn't of course be aware that I had been to both Uptoncester and Hutton Green and knew all about that bunch of grapes. What he did know—as immediately appeared—was the raw fact of the kidnap.

'And now the two boys,' he said. 'A fellow from Scotland Yard came to see me yesterday, and told me what you, no doubt, know already. He told me he was making routine enquiries upon the instructions of some big wig in the police. They'd gathered I'd been to see my nephew here just before he went off with the other lad. So they thought I might be able to throw some light on the matter. I had to say I was only too sorry that I could not. A kidnapping! It's too dreadful. My poor sister!'

I didn't trust myself to speak.

'I doubt,' Tandem said, 'whether that old fellow Daviot has a penny—or not the sort of penny that is relevant in an affair like this. I felt I had to go carefully—very carefully, indeed.'

Again I said nothing. For a moment, even, the man's train of thought was obscure to me.

'It's a form of criminal activity,' Tandem went on, 'that has been developing abroad. I hear about such things.' He hesitated upon this, almost as if he had made some injudicious statement. 'In Italy, for example. The Mafia go in for it. And the key point, Syson, is this: situations develop in which the interests of a family either differ from those of the police or there has to be a pretence that they do so. Of course, it isn't always people that are abducted. Works of art are just as good. Better, in some ways. They don't, after a fashion, have to be fed. And they're easier to keep an eye on.'

'And don't suffer,' I said. 'There's a point there.'

'Perfectly true—not that I'd thought of it. Have you noticed, in reading about such things, how often stolen works of art just turn up unharmed in an inconsequent way in a barn or a left-luggage place or a public lavatory? With the police, as likely as not, taking great credit for their recovery. There's not much difficulty there, since the ransom money comes in a quiet way from an insurance company or even from a Ministry of Fine Arts, or the like. With people—a couple of boys, say, as in the present instance—it's rather different. A schoolboy isn't as important as a Rembrandt or a Titian. So there's no public money ever so privately available.'

Tandem was speaking confidently now: very much the man who knows. I had to sit and watch him eating my ham and drinking my claret.

'Where does this take us?' I asked.

'It takes us to a position in which a victim's relatives and friends want to pay up, and the whole legal establishment—in this country it would be the police and the law officers of the

Crown—are dead against that sort of giving in. Or the authorities try to exploit the appearance of giving in to set a trap for the kidnappers. There can be a real conflict of interests.'

'Yes,' I said—thus offering anything like acquiescence for the first time. I could see that Jasper Tandem, nasty as I obstinately thought him, did know what he was talking about. 'So what happens?'

'Sometimes the family or friends get the money through in spite of any resistance that is put up. They may achieve their bargain. On the other hand, the kidnapped person may have been a corpse for weeks.'

'I can see the risk.'

'Well, these chaps are after money—big money.' Tandem paused on this, and to an effect of considerable emphasis. 'Not a doubt of it. And it's almost impossible, as I've said, that Daviot has a penny. So you see how it may be Robin who is at the centre of the picture, after all. My sister, needless to say, hasn't a bean either. But I'm the boy's uncle, and it's the common belief that I have. So I thought I must explain something to you, Syson. Knowing you have been such a good friend to the lad.'

'I don't think I quite understand you, Mr Tandem,' I said—probably the more stonily because it wasn't quite true. I had a fair notion of what was coming.

'The fact is—and I hope you'll regard it as very much in confidence . . .'

'Mr Tandem, I cannot agree to accept confidences. The situation makes anything of the kind wholly inappropriate. Whatever you tell me I will consider myself as at liberty to communicate, should I judge it desirable, to the police. And I am already in contact with them.'

This brought the man momentarily to a halt. But then he nodded with impressive decision.

'Quite right,' he said. 'I withdraw the condition, and only ask you to be discreet. And now for the plain fact. Anxious though I might be to put up the money in a quiet way, it simply would not be possible. Like Dogberry in the play'—and Tandem produced an unattractive smile at this elegant Shakespearian allusion—'I have had losses. My affairs are very seriously embarrassed.'

155

'I find it the more surprising, then, that you should have wantonly given your nephew that very large sum of money.'

This shook the man, and I suddenly saw that my notion of his being a guest and not to be upbraided was a piece of antique nonsense.

'Robin told you about it?' he asked.

'Nothing of the kind. The amount on the cheque happened to be observed—no doubt as being in a bold hand. I can't say more than that. But it was grossly irresponsible. It was encouraging the boy to behave in a foolish way at a time when he happened to be much upset. It was contemptible, just as is your anxiety to avoid involvement in the wretched situation you envisage. And now you will no doubt wish to leave my house.'

'Just one moment.' Understandably, Jasper Tandem had turned pale. 'It was perhaps injudicious, particularly as I could ill afford the money. I just wanted the boy to have a good time during his half-term break.'

'And I suppose you wanted your brother-in-law to have that when you smuggled more money into Hutton Green. Incidentally, that was a criminal offence.'

Blessedly, the man was now on his feet. (He had finished both claret and ham.) I took some satisfaction in the thought that I was about to turn him out into the snow. A glance through the window revealed that a blizzard was developing. Another couple of hours, it struck me, and Heynoe and all Helmingham might be snowed up. It was true that the school owned a snow-plough which had once cleared a whole hockey-field amid tremendous applause—promptly dashed when the ground was declared too hard for safe play. It seems unlikely that the reminiscence came to me at just that moment. What did come to me was the appalling thought that, with a little ill luck, I might have been landed with a stranded Jasper Tandem for hours or even days.

He took his leave—but it wasn't before having recovered aplomb. Not Mr Pecksniff himself (to switch from Shakespeare to Dickens) could have withdrawn from a discomfiting encounter to a larger effect of rational benignity and a slightly wounded consciousness of merit aspersed. As I watched the

Daimler make an uncertain effort to gain traction and then depart smoothly enough down my drive, I expected to find myself indulging the luxury of extreme indignation. But this didn't happen. Instead, I was conscious only of being increasingly puzzled. Puzzlement, of course, was now the order of my day, the Hayes/Daviot affair being mysterious in every direction—mysterious as well as horrible. But about Robin's uncle there was something especially unaccountable. The cheque, and the banknotes under Messrs Fortnum and Mason's grapes, I continued to find not really bewildering. Sheer delight in malicious contrivance could account for them. But supposing that he really were so despicably enslaved to his own larger financial interests as to panic at the possibility of having to pay out big ransom-money for his nephew, what could prompt him to make a journey to Helmingham to protest his penury to me—who, although in one aspect deeply involved, was only peripheral to the family's problem? I could find no answer to this question. I was left with a groping sense that his purpose had been to put something on record, but that it was a something other than it had purported to be. I could hardly have come up with a notion more nebulous than this. It left my mind as blank and void as was the whitened, the obliterated landscape outside my windows.

# XII

IN THE MIDDLE of the following morning Miss Sparrow turned up on me. The trains, she explained, were still running, although to any sort of chaotic timetable, and she had walked from the nearest railway station. There was nothing like brisk walking, she said, to keep the blood in circulation. As the station was five miles away, and walking can scarcely be brisk when it is through snow eight inches deep and drifting into the bargain, I judged this to be a stout effort on Miss Sparrow's part. Her holiday milieu had in any case threatened boredom, she went on, and in present conditions it had occurred to her that there might be one or two things to do. The women upon whom we relied in the village might be refusing to budge if unprovided with a tractor or snow-shoes, and there were all those beds to change. It was fortunate our sixty-odd boys were snugly at home, since at Heynoe they would be an infernal nuisance if the electricity failed. This was indisputable. Heynoe was without its own generator (a circumstance over which I had known clever prospective fathers shake their heads) and when breakdowns occurred (as they were already doing in those years when the weather turned even a shade unreliable) we were at once down to oil-stoves and candles. (It was the insurance company that shook its head over this.)

'And what about Hayes and Daviot?' Miss Sparrow asked with a briskness that failed to mask her concern.

'There's very bad news,' I said. And I told her the whole thing.

'I see one small satisfaction in it,' Miss Sparrow declared. 'It explains the inexplicable.'

'As a crumb of comfort, I think rather poorly of that.'

'Well, yes—but I do like to think of Robin Hayes as essentially a sensible boy.'

'I think you've said that before.'

'No doubt. But it's important. Bound to have second thoughts quickly. And to act on them, even if still besotted with that silly little Daviot. As it was, he was overtaken by events.'

'Yes.' I didn't much like 'events'. 'And now the police have to discover where and when and how and why.'

'Just that. Are they going to keep us posted?'

'I suppose so. There was this man Ogilvy who is presumably in charge. He seems to regard me as fairly reliable, despite the frightful fool I made of myself in that hotel.'

'Oh, that! I'd have got in just the same fix.' Miss Sparrow took a good look at me. 'You'd better settle down and write letters or something. I've got those beds.' And she left me.

Hard upon this my telephone rang. I had to force myself to take up the receiver. My imagination suggested to me that I was going to hear of something dire beyond conceiving: news of two dead bodies, perhaps, found in a ditch.

'Ogilvy,' a voice said. 'Is that Syson?'

'Yes—Syson.'

'Do you mind having your telephone monitored? I've just arranged the same thing with your headmaster and your colleague Taplow.'

'That's all right.' I had only an indistinct idea of what the man was talking about.

'There are circumstances in which it might save a few valuable minutes. There's been a development.'

'You've discovered something?'

'Not exactly that. But anything's useful. It's nothing at all that we'd really have to worry about.'

It took me a moment to decipher this grammatical ambiguity.

'The villains are now in a hurry, Syson, and that's in our favour. The judge has had his wrist-watch.'

'His wrist-watch? In heaven's name . . .'

'His equivalent of the Hayes wrist-watch. Through the post, and in a shoe-box. Unnaturally light. Daviot, who's decidedly shattered, kept on saying that to me. Unnaturally light. But not when you know what it contained. Locks.'

'Locks? Why should locks be light?'

'Not that sort. Golden locks. And curly.'

'David Daviot!'

'It seems so. I've checked with Taplow, just in case the old gentleman was imagining his grandson's hair to be as it isn't. Shaved, we think, rather than just clipped.' Ogilvy didn't pause to let me respond to this. 'What about you? Anything to report?'

'I'm afraid not. Except that yesterday I had a visit from my boy's uncle—that fellow Tandem. I can't think why. It seemed quite pointless.'

'Pointless?' Ogilvy's voice had sharpened, 'I specialize in pointlessness. It interests me. What pointless things had the man to say? Tell me.'

It would have been easy to find this coolness of tone abrasive. But at once I did my best.

'He was chiefly on about money. If there was any move to pay a big ransom for the boys, he couldn't himself do anything about it. His affairs are embarrassed. But I had a queer feeling he hadn't come down here to exhibit himself in such a disgusting light. Why should he? I felt he felt'—I stumbled over the inelegance of this—'that he was lying about something quite other than his pretended impecuniosity. It was most perplexing.'

'I'd call it most significant, Syson. We'll have a little research done in that quarter. A word, by the way, about the press.'

'The press, Ogilvy?'

'The newspapers. We're not giving out anything at the moment about this kidnapping having happened. But we may be forced to by the villains themselves. In fact they may drop the information of their achievement into the letter-boxes of Fleet Street at any moment. Their motive will be to start showing the police as baffled—a good journalistic word—and to stir up public anxiety. The sooner your fears become public property and generate sinister speculations and sensational headlines, the more quickly will your nerve break and leave you willing to treat. Or so I'd imagine. It's all rather new ground, you know.

160

Not many case-histories to compare it with. But even if the villains keep mum, we can't sit on the thing, announcement-wise, for long. Perhaps another twenty-four hours. Well, that's it. We mustn't be too glum. The situation's grim, of course. But not desperate. Good-bye.'

I ate some bread and cheese, and then took Miss Sparrow's advice and tried to write some letters. The effort didn't achieve much. My mind turned from one perplexity to another. Ogilvy had added to them with his information that the police were seeking to delay giving out the news of what had happened to the two boys, and it was some time before I hit on the full and sinister explanation. The sense that a hunt was up, if it caught the criminals with their dispositions only in part achieved, might rattle them and imperil the safety of their captives. It must be something like that. It wasn't a comforting thought, and I was digesting it when my front-door bell rang. As I had done with Tandem on the previous day, I answered it myself. This time my visitor was a young man, and unknown to me.

'Good afteroon,' he said politely. 'Mr Syson?'

'Yes.'

'I wonder, sir, whether I might come in and have a word with you?'

I couldn't very well have said, 'Certainly not', but I could at least have asked him his business before letting him cross my doorstep. Unfortunately I was less suspicious than I ought to have been. I think I supposed him to be some representative of a firm publishing school-books, to be listened to civilly for a few minutes and then bowed out. So I led the way into my study. Once there, the young man sat down at once.

'The name's Kilpin,' he said. 'And I'm afraid I'm only from the *Gazette*.' The *Gazette* was our harmless local rag. 'I wondered whether . . .'

'I am afraid, Mr Kilpin, that I cannot help you.' Now at least I could guess where I stood with this visitor.

'Mr Stafford,' Kilpin went on unheeding, 'has been good enough to talk to me once or twice in the past, but today he is unfortunately unavailable for comment. So I thought I'd try you, sir. Being the housemaster—if that's the word—of one of those lads. A couple of pars in humorous vein is what I'd be thinking of. Our readers, you know, are always interested in a bit of light stuff about a great school like Helmingham.' Kilpin appeared to feel he might safely pause for a space on this, since it conveyed a handsome compliment. So I had a moment to think. I mustn't, I saw, react too vigorously to his impertinent intrusion, since I might thereby simply provide him with a little gratuitous copy. And I saw something else. The man could be only scantily informed of what had happened, since a couple of pars in humorous vein could scarcely be concocted on the theme of criminal abduction. So the police silence held, and here was a more or less harmless annoyance. Nevertheless it must be ended at once.

'Taken French leave, haven't they?' Kilpin said agreeably. 'A funny phrase, that. It's because in France they leave parties without a thank-you-kindly. I'm interested in such things, Mr Syson, language being important to a journalist, as you'll agree. German measles, French letters, Dutch elm disease—that's a new one.' Kilpin paused again, and apparently saw that this philological discourse failed to enchant me. 'But to business,' he said. 'A bit of a lark, it sounds to be, on the part of Master Hayes and Master Daviot. It wouldn't be exactly what you call a rag. A prank, perhaps. Might I have a few words on it from you, Mr Syson?'

'Definitely not, Mr Kilpin. I have nothing to say to you.'

'But you'll have something to say to those two when they turn up again, I don't doubt. And something to do to them as well. Six of the best, will it be? May I put that down, Mr Syson—six of the best?'

At this I was tempted to tell myself that it would be pleasurable to come at Mr Kilpin with a belt. I contented myself, however, with rapidly crossing my study and opening the door.

'Mr Kilpin,' I said, 'I have no doubt that you are exercising your profession in a perfectly proper way. I make no complaint. But I am sorry I must say good-afternoon to you. Just how, by the way, did you come by your information?'

162

'Servants, Mr Syson. Servants will talk—particularly if stood a drink or two in a pub. I don't like it.' Kilpin remained entirely amiable; he even seemed gratified that I had run to a question myself. 'It's demeaning, sir, I don't deny. But first steps, you see. A man must walk before he can run, if I may coin a phrase. Investigative journalism is what I aim at, Mr Syson. It's something there's a big future in. Very much obliged for your co-operation.'

And Mr Kilpin withdrew—no doubt with his couple of pars already formed in his mind. When I returned to my study, it was to answer yet another telephone call.

'Syson, come over here at once.'

'Certainly, Head Master.' To receive a command or instruction rather than a request or suggestion from John Stafford was altogether unusual, and at least suggested that he was as worried as anybody else. 'I'll come immediately.'

'The noble six hundred'—it was thus that Stafford occasionally designated the school as a body—'will be back with us in no time, and there are problems ahead. I've got Taplow here. Yours are the two houses chiefly concerned.'

'Certainly they are. I'll very much value your help.'

With this politic speech I hung up, and got into an overcoat. Even so, the walk through the grounds was a chilly business. The two men were drinking tea. Tim Taplow was looking gloomy. Stafford had very much the air of the man at the helm.

'It mayn't have occurred to you, Syson,' he said, 'but for a start we may probably have the press to contend with.'

'Yes, so we may.' Whether I got anything of what Robin Hayes would have called irony into this, I don't know. 'I've been trying to understand the police wanting to keep mum for a bit. They say the criminals themselves may come out with what they've achieved at any moment, but that they themselves don't yet want to. It's puzzling.'

'The criminals *have* come out with it,' Taplow said. 'To both Hayes's mother and the judge.'

'Yes, of course.' Stafford was impatient. 'But they may believe that Mrs Hayes is still no more than bewildered—and distracted by her husband's exploit into the bargain. And they can't be certain that the judge isn't keeping silent and thinking of coming to terms with them in a private deal.'

'Daviot is certainly doing nothing of the kind,' I said. 'He started in on Scotland Yard and the Home Secretary and lord knows who almost before his grandson's disappearance became alarming. His paranoiac strain, you know. And he disclosed the arrival of that unspeakable parcel at once.'

'Perfectly true.' Stafford took this up incisively. 'But this fellow Ogilvy—I gather he has been in contact with you, Syson—seems to believe in some kind of war of nerves. I get the impression that he has no high opinion of the average criminal intelligence—which may well be a mistake—and feels that keeping a low profile—an odd expression, to be sure—may lure them into some false step. Puzzle them, and they'll commit themselves to something that gives them away. We can only hope he's right.'

'I take it,' Taplow said, 'that our trouble is this: in no time we're going to have several hundred boys all agog to know what has become of Robert's Head of House and his curly-headed little chum. And if we keep mum it mayn't greatly help us that we are acting on police advice. I can even imagine, Head Master, the School Governors being eventually a little worried about it.'

This was at once an untimely and an implausible shaft, and I thought poorly of it. But it did no more than show that we were considerably shaken. Stafford, I thought, must be shaken if he really believed that the reassembling of the school after the half-term break constituted a problem anywhere near the heart of the matter. Inevitably it was the reputation of Helmingham that stood first in his mind, and he saw the whole shocking business, I suppose, in terms of degrees of scandal. Just why had the two boys run away? What were they running away from? If public attention were directed in this direction, the consequences might no doubt be uncomfortable. I was almost startled to find how little I myself seemed to be bothering about this. It might have been put that there were five hundred and ninety eight boys that I didn't care tuppence for. There were two that I cared about very much.

This idle thought hadn't time to grow, and I was never to know how Stafford received Taplow's remark. For the telephone had rung—only this one discreetly buzzed—on his large and always impressively burdened desk.

He picked up the instrument. He said 'Yes'. He listened, and said 'Yes' again. Then he listened silently for some time. It is impossible to be the part-auditor of an exchange of this sort without a sensation of awkwardness. Taplow and I tried muttering to one another in an unattending way. But then Stafford said firmly that it had occurred to him as a hopeful line of enquiry, and that his colleagues were with him and that he would tell them at once. After a further interval he said, 'Thank you very much', and hung up the receiver. He turned to us.

'Ogilvy,' he said. 'He is most punctiliously keeping us informed. They've traced the taxi.'

'The taxi?' I asked, and immediately felt extremely stupid.

'The taxi that the boys drove away in. They took it right across country to some inconsiderable station on a branch line. That has held things up a little. But now the police have located a booking-clerk who remembers them. Two lads, one a good deal older than the other. They bought a couple of second-class singles. To Uptoncester.'

# XIII

So Miss Sparrow had been right, and Iain Macleod, although Robin's closest friend, had got it wrong. Not Morocco or California, but Uptoncester. Whatever calamity had happened there, I ought to have experienced a certain relief in this discovery. Miss Sparrow had expressed faith in the boy's basic common sense, and here was the admirable woman's judgement vindicated. With whatever extravagance, whatever wounding rhetoric to myself the flight from Helmingham had been accompanied, its good-hearted character on Robin's part was now established. Discovering or imagining young David Daviot to be in a horrible situation, he had simply decided to carry him off to his own home, his mother and his sister—from which refuge he no doubt intended, as Miss Sparrow had conjectured, to open negotiations with Sir Henry Daviot to secure the boy's permanent removal from School House. There hadn't been much knowledge of the world and its ways in the manoeuvre, but at least it had been unselfish and honourable.

It is a curious fact that at this juncture I have to record in myself an irrational tinge of disappointment. I can find no very secure explanation of this. Was it the issue of a kind of smothered romanticism lurking unsuspected in my own heart? Could I conceivably have felt anything alluringly romantic in the notion of those two ignorant boys attempting a get-away beyond the bounds of respectable society? A mere fleeting fantasy of the kind was thoroughly disturbing. I hurried back through the snow from the Head Master's house to Heynoe, intent on giving the news—good so far as it went—to my sagacious Matron. I was half-way there before there returned to my mind with any force the remaining and overpowering horror of the affair. That dull house in its quiet crescent had been a goal unachieved.

Somewhere on their route to it the boys had vanished, had fallen into the hands of abominable criminals.

Miss Sparrow received my communication without surprise, and even with a slight impatience which was odd until she explained herself.

'There has been a message for you,' she said. 'A telephone call that I took myself—and from Sir Henry. He would be grateful if he might so far trespass upon your kindness—you remember the way he talks—as to go up to town at once and confer with him.'

'To confer with him?' It came inconsequently into my head that I had been judged to have 'conferred' with Owen Marchmont and Ogilvy. 'Has he invited Stafford and Taplow as well?'

'I think not. It was my impression that he rather regards Robin Hayes as the *clou* to the whole riddle, and judges that you know more about him than anybody else.'

'It's the man being crazy again. Did he sound crazy?'

'Not in the least. Wholly collected and purposeful. And what he seemed to be arranging was a formal meeting with the police authorities in charge of the case.'

'I'd better go.'

'Certainly you had. And I can get you through to the station in my car. With luck you'll catch the fast train.'

I hadn't even got out of my overcoat, and now there was no time to be lost. Bizarre as this unexpected summons to London appeared to be, I found a certain relief in the bustle of it. I worried about the train, estimating the possibility of its being held up by the atrocious weather. But it wasn't so. I got myself (unlike the boys) a first-class ticket, and tumbled into an empty compartment in which, predictably, something had gone wrong with the heating. I wondered whether there was any heating, whether to go wrong or right, in whatever evil place the boys were secreted. And again and again there came back to me, with a sensation as of a sudden blow on the heart, the remoteness of what had happened from any experience I had my bearings in. Around me in a sense, or no further off than a newspaper before my nose, was a world in which not the march of armies or the thunder of cannon, but sporadic small-scale violence was becoming as common as football matches or bad weather. Airliners on their normal occasions were being 'hijacked' over every continent on the globe; 'terrorist' was a term ceasing to belong to French eighteenth-century or Russian nineteenth-century history and was cropping up in every bulletin from the BBC. Merely because one was a law-abiding citizen one had no title to a sense of outrage if coercive violence slapped out at one. These were my reflections as a taxi trundled me up Haverstock Hill to the Hampstead dwelling of Sir Henry Daviot. It was a house upon every lintel of which there might have been incised an assurance of the Queen's peace. But a policeman, too impassive even to stamp his chilly feet, stood on the doorstep.

To this last circumstance the judge almost immediately alluded—and to an effect of slight embarrassment which surprised me.

'Mr Syson, it is very good of you to come up. My car will be round in half an hour, and we will go and see those men at Scotland Yard. I suppose, you know, it must be acknowledged I am getting on, and occasionally subject to not very rational alarms. One of these occasions I know you have witnessed. How erroneously it was conceived, you will presently be made aware of. But there is a shade more substance, perhaps, to what has succeeded it. Hence the presence of that fellow on my doorstep.'

'He did give me a hard look,' I said. 'But he made no move to search me for a bomb.'

Why I indulged this unsuitable levity I don't know. Miss Sparrow's 'collected and purposeful' was a just description of Sir Henry as he now was—which was not at all as I recollected him. Had I been an innocent man in a dock with this judge on the bench in front of me, I'd have had considerable confidence that he would steer things the right way. This change in Daviot may have thrown me out a little.

'First about Hayes,' he said, '—the man who has decamped from that injudiciously conceived prison. Nobody has set eyes on him, you know, so he can't be altogether a fool.'

'I suppose not, Sir Henry.' The judge's speech, as may be imagined, was a considerable relief to me. Sooner or later he was bound to be given an account, even if in terms of Owen Marchmont's tactful doctoring, which would invalidate what he had just said. But at the moment my improper conduct in the Hutton Arms was unknown to him and could occasion no awkwardness between us.

'But that he left Hutton Green in pursuance of some vague design against me is a hypothesis I now unreservedly reject. The fellow is, as the policemen like to say, in the clear, so far as that is concerned. And the same is almost certainly true of his unfortunate son, the boy Robin. Robin's rash conduct may well have been cleverly precipitated by the news of his father's behaviour, but the connection between the two events stops there. It is true that Mr Ogilvy, whom I understand you have met, has given thought to another interpretation of the matter, which would imply the extraordinary postulate that Robin Hayes has been a party to a cunning deception, and is not in fact being held against his will. But I don't believe it, and Ogilvy, a man of wide experience of criminals and their ways, doesn't believe it either.'

'I myself, Sir Henry, judged it incredible from the start.'

'Quite so, Mr Syson, and the fact has had great weight with me. As has the opinion of that sensible woman I met in your company. Miss Wren, I think.'

'Sparrow.'

'Miss Sparrow. You both know the boy. I think it is equally true that I know my grandson. I am deeply attached to David, but I see him in one aspect as a rather vain and gullible child. There is all that nonsense about a theatrical career. But what bearing that may have on the situation must be regarded at present as obscure.'

'Yes.'

'So Robin, poor boy, is also in the clear. And if any harm has come to him, or to my grandson, or to both of them, I think I can assure you that the judiciary will take a severe view of the fact.'

I held my peace before this, the notion of retributive justice seeming to me to carry no comfort whatever. But it was, of course, Sir Henry Daviot's sort of thing.

'And now, Mr Syson, let us turn to Robin Hayes in his family connection. You may have remarked that I was considerably

169

startled to hear that a man called Jasper Tandem is his uncle. Tandem happens to be known to me as not exactly a model citizen. He has had several close shaves, if the truth be told.'

'With the law?' The mild colloquialism in which the judge had indulged startled me a little. I could almost hear discreet mirth in court.

'Certainly. And over a long period of years. When he was a very young man, and I was myself a junior counsel, hard up and practising at the criminal bar, I once tried to see him sent down. I didn't succeed. Nor has anyone else since—although his subsequent life has certainly not been a blameless one. It is conceivable, indeed, that he has been involved in matters putting him uncomfortably in the power of professional criminals.'

'These seem significant circumstances, Sir Henry.'

'They may certainly be that—and you will see why there was a point at which I was disposed to suspect somewhat extensive conspiracy. But at least we here confront a puzzle. Tandem made his nephew that quite extraordinary gift of money. Was it in furtherance of some criminal intent to which the uncle was more or less constrained—and of which the nephew was quite unaware? Was its motive to get the boys into a situation more favourable for abduction than would be afforded while they were secure within a populous boarding-school? That is a question to which you must give the most careful consideration.'

For the moment I could only nod silently. It was as if Mr Justice Daviot had believed himself to be delivering his charge to a jury.

'What I myself pause on,' he continued, 'is the amount of the gift. Indeed, its magnitude would be a reasonable term.'

'It certainly seems to me an unnecessarily large sum for the purpose you are suggesting.'

'But yet, Mr Syson, consider.' Sir Henry raised a hand as if to restrain some headlong speed in my own cogitations. 'Here in young Hayes is a normally level-headed boy—yet usefully (as one may put it) a little off balance as a consequence of the misfortune in his family. Might not the sudden gift of a very large sum of money serve to unbalance him further? I recall his friend who spoke up to me so well. With the Scottish name.'

'Iain Macleod.'

'Yes. When he spoke of Morocco or California it turns out that he was mistaken, so far as Robin Hayes's succeeding conduct was concerned. But it was a good suggestion, all the same. A thousand pounds would serve as a strong prompting to travel far afield. But the escapade, if undertaken, would not get far. The boys would be trapped by the kidnappers upon some early opportunity their folly had created. But that the trap originated with Tandem, one need not believe. He was an agent merely—and perhaps a not wholly willing one at that. Mr Syson, what is your general impression of the man's character?'

'I have been thinking of him in terms of mischief or malice, rather than as one involved in some conspiracy. Anything simply malicious seems to appeal to him. Witness his tempting his brother-in-law to that idiotic breaking out of prison. But I've had no more than a couple of encounters with Tandem. I gather that as a boy he was expelled from his school, and I feel that his attitude to public schools in general has remained mixed ever since. On the one hand nostalgia taking rather tiresome and even unwholesome forms, and on the other resentment and an impulse to make trouble if he can.'

'He may have been forced into making more trouble than he had the stomach for. When did you last see him?'

'It was only yesterday. He paid me a visit at Helmingham that puzzled me a good deal.'

'Just why, Mr Syson?'

'I had an odd feeling that he felt himself to be on the fringe of something dangerous. I told Mr Ogilvy about it on the telephone. He seemed interested.'

'As well he might. Can you be more precise about this impression you received?'

'I don't know that I can, Sir Henry. Tandem was very insistent that he hasn't any money to speak of. It was as if nothing but a sum that might have to be raised was in his head. And I had an unaccountable feeling—again I told Ogilvy about it—that the anxiety he exhibited was in some way spurious.'

171

'It may well have been, if he was playing a double game.' The judge was suddenly grim. 'A worthless fellow.'

'Then why should he turn up on me?'

'Why, indeed? If I may say so, Mr Syson, it is an acute question. And now we had better go and see the police. A good many of them are involved, and the convenient thing will be that we should go to them, rather than the other way round. If you are agreeable.'

'Yes, of course.' I felt that in this last consideration Sir Henry was in a routine way consulting his own dignity. His distress and anxiety were emphasized rather than masked by the stiff control he was exercising over himself.

So we went out to his now-waiting car: a chauffeur-driven affair. The policeman saluted—and then, rather as an afterthought, stepped down and opened the door of the vehicle. The slushy pavements were quite deserted, except for a single figure on the other side of the road. He was peering up at the house-numbers, and had the air of a man trying to find his way about. My glimpse of this struck an odd chord for a moment in my mind. But I gave no further thought to it.

Dusk had been falling during my interview with David Daviot's grandfather. By the time of our arrival at New Scotland Yard what passes for darkness in the heart of London was all around us. We were expeditiously received. I seemed just to glimpse the odd little revolving advertisement in which the place indulges, a large hall, a small memorial to something or other, when I found myself in a lift with Sir Henry and several silent men who appeared to have nothing to do with one another. The lift halted—although without permitting gravity to give us any notice of the fact—and we were shown into a room in which a further half-dozen men were sitting round a table. They stood up to receive us—or rather to receive the judge—but were already seated again and fingering papers before chairs had been found for us. No time was being wasted. And Ogilvy, who was at the head of the table, spoke at once.

'Reports,' he said. 'Detective Superintendent Jefferson.'

Jefferson revealed himself by clearing his throat. He was a

florid man whose principal endowment appeared to me to be a pair of unnaturally piercing light blue eyes. These, I thought, might well have taken him all the way from the beat to his present elevated position in the Metropolitan Police. A single glance from them would surely unnerve the most hardened malefactor.

'Taking things in order, then,' Jefferson said. 'The first event we hear of is the prisoner Hayes escaping from Hutton Green. If escaping it can be called. Some might be in two minds about that.'

'I hope,' Ogilvy said, 'that none of us are presently going to be in two minds over more important matters. Continue.'

'Yes, sir. Next, there's what he does. Crosses the road, as you may say, and puts up in the local pub—a comfortable one, by all accounts. You have to admire that, in a manner of speaking. But you have to learn from it as well.'

'Good,' Ogilvy said.

'Thank you, sir. It's a matter of the cast of mind revealed, isn't it? An eye for the uses of the invisible because sublimely obvious thing.' Jefferson paused on this, and I had leisure to recall Edgar Allan Poe. The Detective Superintendent's criminological studies had perhaps extended to that story of a purloined letter. 'Hayes,' Jefferson continued, 'is flushed out of that pub in a manner that hasn't quite been made clear to me. So where does he go? Home. The obvious answer is Home. Of course it's no more than a notion. Or *was* no more than a notion. But worth investigating.'

'Eminently,' Ogilvy said.

'Thank you, sir. Of course we've had that house in Uptoncester fairly closely watched from the first. It has been very cold, it seems, down there. Colder by a long way than here in London. So people have been going about huddled up.' Jefferson paused on this. 'Huddled up,' he repeated with an air of muted drama—and directed those intimidating eyes in a baleful manner upon an officer sitting across the table from him. 'Of course it was local men who were keeping Hayes's house under observation. And what one of them saw was a huddled-up figure coming down the road carrying what you might call a bill-board or scratch-pad. Stopping and ringing the bells at every house, and going into some of them. Reading the meters, he might have been, or working for one of those opinion polls. And this local Vidocq wasn't much interested in him. Isn't even sure whether he entered Hayes's house. Or, for that matter, came out again. Only some dim thought about it came to him later on.'

'I've always regarded him as a very responsible officer,' the man who had been glared at said gruffly. 'Of course I've had the surveillance tightened up, and nobody will now come out without being questioned. I've had instructions to be very chary about seeming to harass the ladies of the house. Mr Ogilvy, I hope you will corroborate that.'

'Certainly,' Ogilvy said. 'So there Hayes Senior may be—and out of the way of further mischief. And there, for the moment, we can leave him. I doubt whether he's very near the hard core of the affair. So carry on, Mr Jefferson, to your next performer.'

At this moment a uniformed man entered the room and handed Ogilvy a note. Raising a delaying hand, Ogilvy read it with what I judged to be increasingly studied composure. He then wrote a note himself, with which the uniformed man left the room. 'Yes, Jefferson?' Ogilvy said.

'The next man, sir, would be Tandem. Hayes's brother-in-law, that is.'

'Ah, yes—Tandem.' Ogilvy appeared to come to a decision. 'One interesting thing about Tandem most of you haven't yet heard about. He has been declaring himself as very apprehensive that a demand for ransom money may arrive on his doorstep, since it will be believed that he is the wealthy member of the family. Well, I've just heard'—and Ogilvy tapped the note still in front of him—'what may relieve him of that anxiety. The kidnappers have moved again—and we can account ourselves lucky that they now feel in such a devil of a hurry. They've made their demand, but not to Mr Tandem. They've made it to the Lord Chancellor—or to his office, to be more exact.'

'The Lord Chancellor!' It was now for the first time that Sir Henry Daviot spoke. He sounded less dumbfounded than

174

scandalized. 'In heaven's name what has Lord Hailsham to do with the abduction of my grandson and his companion?'

'What, indeed. But, Sir Henry, may I put a question to you?'

'Certainly.'

'Does the name Kilroy convey anything to you?'

'No.'

'Or Kissack, or Hudson?'

'I think not. But names come and go.'

'Precisely. And the owners of these three have two things in common. They are all now in gaol. And it was you who sent them down.'

'And the demand?'

'Yes, Sir Henry. It's not for money. It's for men.'

This was a bombshell. It was rather as if an actual bomb had gone off in the big hall many floors below us. Or, more exactly, it was as if news had been received of rabies having crossed the English Channel. This was something which, commonly in a political context, was already happening in distant countries of which we knew little. Here, it was, I imagine, virtually a 'first'. Robin Hayes and David Daviot were to be released from bondage if three common criminals were let out of gaol.

My own heart sank as the implications of this came home to me. Recently at the back of my head had been the possibility that, in a last resort, the law might turn a blind eye to some actual ransom being unobtrusively arranged. But now the kidnappers were revealed as having acted in ghastly ignorance, making a demand to which, surely, no English government would submit. I wondered confusedly whether I was right about this. I glanced at Daviot and imagined that I saw my conviction mirrored on his face. And then I heard Ogilvy speaking again.

'So here is progress, gentlemen. Let us be clear about that. An hour ago we had nothing, or almost nothing, although we weren't saying so even among ourselves. Now we have the names of these three men in gaol; and somewhere is a group of their associates who are mounting this caper. They must be close associates, and with loyalty enough to venture such a desperate game. The criminal records of those three—Kilroy, Kissack, Hudson—are certain to yield a lead on some of them. The files are being sifted through now.'

'They must be reckoning on that,' somebody said. 'The villains must. That naming those names gives us some sort of line on them. They'll have taken precautions accordingly.'

'Perfectly true. Here's our chance, all the same.'

With this, the meeting broke up—the affair having moved, as it were, into another gear. I wondered whether Ogilvy was putting a bold face on a desperate situation. Supposing a real trail were established, and the kidnappers knew the hunt was hot behind them: what would they then do with the two boys? Would they free them, and themselves simply make a run for it? Or would some more evil and vengeful course attract them? I thought—stupidly, no doubt, and in a fashion which liberal-minded persons will at once condemn—that it was a pity no image of a gallows could influence their deliberations.

Sir Henry Daviot invited me home for the night, but I distrusted our present ability to be of any support to one another. I went instead to a married sister in Kensington, who took entirely in her stride my unheralded arrival without so much as a toothbrush. In the course of perhaps an hour's sleep I had a dream characterized by acute anxiety. This was unsurprising. But in it I found myself to be one of the companions of Hernando Cortés during his dreadful march from Mexico to Honduras in 1524, an episode about which I must have read in Prescott's book when an undergraduate. This is of no significance for my narrative—unless, indeed, the useless behaviour of my mind in sleep prompted me to seek something to be useful about when awake. I ate a hasty breakfast, thanked my sister and brother-in-law for their hospitality, and caught an early train to Uptoncester.

# XIV

GLANCING BACK OVER these pages, I find that I have accorded too much space to what was passing through my own head as the various events transacted themselves. Nevertheless, I make one final pause in the same interest now. Ogilvy and his team had impressed me, although I doubt whether I have managed to make them seem particularly impressive. The mere discovery that it appeared to have been for Robin's home that the ill-fated boys had set out was no great achievement in itself. That rapid research into the activities and associations of three men named Kilroy, Kissack and Hudson would turn the tables on the kidnappers was a persuasion that remained to be proved. But I understood something of the excitement of the chase, and was even a little resentful that I had no part in it. My presence at the conference in Scotland Yard had been due merely to a whim on the judge's part, and I had been accommodated at it with civility. But my active rôle in the story had been small and was now over, securely docketed in appropriate police notebooks. So what of any relevance could I find to do?

The answer to this question had come to me in the form of a fairly vivid sense of the state of affairs now obtaining in the Hayes household. Mr Hayes, that surprisingly resourceful if thoroughly tiresome character, had contrived to return to its shelter—and no doubt believed that he had done so undetected. The police for the moment were uninterested in him: a minor figure usefully out of the way, to be picked up with a considerate unobtrusiveness later. But what, meanwhile, was the state of mind of his wife and daughter? They must both be conscious of the escaped man's folly—and his wife was probably very cross about it. Neither, it seemed, had cleared her mind and hardened her heart to the extent of communicating with the local police.

The position of Mrs Hayes—impossible woman though she was—struck me as particularly difficult. A person in the Queen's commission, she was actually harbouring a fugitive from one of Her Majesty's prisons. It seemed to me that the ladies ought to have some masculine support in their predicament, and that this I might myself afford them. My first visit had not been a great success, but I might do better on a second.

Looking back now, I can see the notion as an absurdity. Yet it was powerful with me at the time, and had put me on the train for Uptoncester.

Failing to find much of interest in a newspaper, I spent most of the journey looking out of the window. It was at a countryside now deeply blanketed in snow, and with villages, farms, stations, big roads, little roads alike appearing curiously dispeopled. It was as if under the sudden assault of winter the entire human race had lost its nerve and dodged under blankets of a more comfortable sort while thinking out a strategy for survival through freezing weeks ahead. We were clearly in for one of those frequently recurring winters the like of which we are told has not been seen for many years.

In Uptoncester itself the effect was very similar. A white leprosy or Black Death might have annihilated its inhabitants. In the station yard, never exactly a bustling place, I looked in vain for a taxi—or even (what still existed in such places) a horse-drawn cab. Turning up the collar of my overcoat, I went ahead on foot and with considerable caution. Some stretches of pavement had been cleared of snow, and some had not. But whether exposed or treacherously lurking beneath the slush, there appeared to be everywhere a film of ice. A little snow was actually falling—and no sooner had I observed this than the few flakes turned into a blizzard. There was not, indeed, much wind to blow this about. So the stuff came straight down as if in an altogether inordinate hurry to join the great carpeting of it below. I have already had to record one instance of my rapidly losing all sense of direction under similarly adverse weather, and the same thing happened to me now. What I could see of Uptoncester's landmarks perplexingly shifted ground even as I uncertainly glimpsed them. I came to a crossroads and hadn't a clue as to whether to turn to my right or my left.

But I wasn't, it seemed, the only person at a loss, since even as I hesitated a vehicle drew to a halt beside me. I had an impression of the sort of post-office van which has been turned over to private ownership, and then a man was leaning out of its open window and waving a piece of paper at me.

'Excuse me, mate,' he called out. 'Can you tell me where I'll find . . .?'

And this was all I either heard or saw. For suddenly the universe appeared to crash down on my head. I don't think that, for the moment, I felt any pain at all. I had been knocked senseless on the instant—there in the deserted heart of the quiet cathedral town.

When I regained consciousness it was my first hazy conviction that I was being trundled through darkness on a wheel-barrow. The process was uncomfortably bumpy. I rolled over awkwardly, and my head—which was painful anyway—knocked painfully against metal. I put out an arm to steady myself. Or rather I tried to do this and failed. The arm wouldn't move. The horrifying thought came to me that I had slipped on that treacherous ice and come down so heavily as to paralyse one of my limbs—or all of them. It *was* all of them. I was helpless. But I was helpless because I was tied up.

'Not so cocky now, mate?' My attempt at movement had been detected, and a voice spoke from the front of the van. For it was a van. I now remembered the van. And the van wasn't after all entirely dark. There was a little grid through which light filtered, and through which the voice had come. 'Incompetent, all you fuzz,' the voice went on tolerantly. 'Thought we hadn't spotted you snooping around where you had no call to be t'other day? And again with that judge yesterday? And here you are today too? Shit! On leave you are now, mate. Furlough, as they say. The longest holiday you're like to have for a long time. And don't try hollering, or you'll get quite a surprise. And you know where. Put it in often enough yourself, I'll be bound. Bloody Pig.'

I realized, without amusement, that I was believed to be a policeman, and that I was a captive in the same hands as were Robin Hayes and David Daviot. I made no attempt to holler. There might well be two men in front, and one might come into the back and pleasantly deal with me while the other simply drove on. There was nothing for it. I was booked for prison—and not an open one, either.

After this there was silence. It was my impression that the drive went on for a very long time and traversed varying ground. Sometimes there was the noise of other traffic, as if we were in an urban area. At other times there was the silence of what must be open country. Once or twice I thought I distinguished—and it was a strangely eerie effect—the faint bleating of sheep, the contented lowing of cattle. Perhaps we were on our way to some country retreat of the criminals across the breadth of England.

I tried to think coherently. The risky part of their exploit must have been at the moment of capturing me in Uptoncester. Even through that convenient blizzard, their action might by some chance have been detected. This must have been even more true of the first kidnapping. It, too, had presumably happened in Uptoncester, since it had been for Uptoncester that the boys had taken train. Perhaps they had arrived there after dark. But how had the criminals known of and seized their opportunity? Here was a mystery. And where would they then make for? Bundling the captives out of this van or a similar vehicle and into their prison was a manoeuvre they could better control. That, certainly, would happen in the dark—or if not in the dark wholly within private property screened from casual observation. I was the next parcel and would be similarly dealt with. Perhaps I wasn't being driven over great distances, but only round and round until darkness fell. I had a sense that this conjecture pointed forward to another one. But I couldn't make out what it was. My head was still working not at all well. Perhaps my brain had been damaged for good.

This sort of dismal rigmarole terminated abruptly when abruptly the van came to a halt. It hadn't, so far as I could remember, done so even once before—which suggested that we couldn't have been through anything like a town with numerous traffic lights. This useless piece of detective-work was my last before the door at the back of the van was flung open. I had a glimpse of wintry sunshine and of three men positioned alertly in front of me. Then instantly something—a bag or blanket—was flung over my head, and I was hauled and heaved I didn't know where. Moments later I was dropped, neither viciously nor gently, on what must have been a bare stone or concrete floor. Very briefly there were voices, then the sound of a heavy door closing, and after that I thought I heard, although I couldn't be certain, the van or another vehicle driving away.

'*Cold.*'

The word—but it was half word and half sob or snivel—came out of a darkness that was not quite entire. The bag or blanket must have been removed from my head—positively as an act of courtesy, it was possible to feel—and a world of faint shadows was around me.

'*Cold.*'

I wondered about my bonds, and found I was still in some fashion tethered to myself, although I couldn't yet quite make out how.

'*Cold.*'

It was certainly very cold indeed. I was already registering the fact, so that the reiterated assertion was unnecessary and also frightening.

'*So cold.*'

'*S-s-sh!*' This, a sharp low command, came from my other side. So there was a third in my dungeon, and I knew very well who both my companions were. 'Who's that?' the second voice—Robin's voice—whispered. 'Who's there?'

'Robin, it's me: Robert Syson. They've caught me too.'

'Whyever . . .?' The single word revealed Robin Hayes as strained, exhausted, but in command of himself as the unfortunate younger boy was not.

'They've taken me for a snooping policeman. I was prowling around Uptoncester some days ago—and again today. If it still *is* today.' I paused to collect myself. 'Robin, we're not gagged. Is it no good shouting?'

'*I'm cold.*'

'Definitely not. I've tried. Sammy just comes and clobbers you. Sammy has some other nasty tricks as well. But Sammy's soft, all the same.'

'Soft?' The word seemed to echo something I'd heard from Owen Marchmont aeons before.

'I'm hoping so. I'm working on him. I'd like to work on him the way he has once or twice worked on me. But it's cajolement that's the thing. Every dishonest promise I can think of. I believe he's stupid. Or I hope he is.'

'Is he the only one on guard?'

'I think so—sometimes. I think the others go away to feed. Fat of the land, probably. Sammy's lowly—just their hey-you. *He* feeds *us*. After a fashion. From time to time. It's not the bloody Ritz.'

'I suppose not.' I felt Robin to be speaking out of a forlorn hope. But I was thanking heaven for him, all the same.

'*I'm so cold.*'

'David, belt up for a bit. Mr Syson, I apologize.'

'You *what*, Robin?'

'For the way I spoke to you. I was a bit off my head.'

'We must forget about it. But, Robin, tell me all you can about what happened. Was that uncle of yours . . .?'

'It did begin, in a way, with wicked Uncle Jasper. He tanked me up well, didn't he? And there was masses of money, and this marvellous plan. David and I would really show the flag. Go off to heaven knows where. Timbuctoo, perhaps. But, for a start, just to a small, out-of-the-way country pub.'

'I see.' I felt I did see—and thought it just a further touch of the bizarre that there would thus have been two Hayeses lurking in pubs simultaneously. 'But you thought better of it?'

'Of course. I don't, you know, go all that dippy for all that long. So I decided just to take David home with me, and then get at that grandfather of his and tell him about the goings on . . .'

'In School House. All that, Robin. But those people nabbed you both, all the same—even although you didn't go to that out-of-the-way pub?'

'Yes, in Uptoncester itself. They have a nerve. I give them that. And luck.'

'You realize that your uncle must be—well, one of them?'

'Not quite that, I think. They just have a hold on him. A pretty stiff hold from dubious episodes in times past. Something like that.'

'But he *can't* have intended that his own nephew . . .'

'Well, perhaps he thought they'd only take David, and not bother with me. I just don't know. You haven't seen him lately, have you?'

'*Cold.*'

'Yes, I have. He called on me again in Heynoe—pretending to know less of what it was all about than he actually did.'

'About those people wanting money?'

'They don't, Robin—although your uncle was out to persuade me he believed it was that. He was trying to distance himself from the whole thing. What those people really want is to exchange the two of you—and now, I suppose, me—not for ransom money but for some of their friends who are in gaol.'

'That just couldn't happen, could it?'

Robin's voice as he asked this was perfectly steady. And I gave an honest answer.

'No,' I said. 'I don't think it could.'

This cautiously half-whispered conversation between us went on for some time. David Daviot, although he had ceased his plaint, made no contribution to it. Perhaps he had fallen asleep. I was even more sorry for David, to whom I had never spoken, than for Robin. Robin had his sustaining plan. I wasn't sanguine about it, but was as yet without material for a fair judgement.

After what was perhaps a couple of hours, this deficiency began to be made good. A door opened and there was a chink of light. The beam from an electric torch was at play on us each in turn. It wavered a little during the process, as if held in a not quite steady hand. Through its faintly diffused radiance I had an uncertain glimpse of the man called Sammy. He seemed a meagre little creature—not at all what is known in the underworld as a heavy.

'Hullo, Sammy,' Robin said cheerfully.

'Hullo yourself.' Sammy's immediate note was of a kind of jocular truculence which somehow revealed a good deal. He wasn't quite up to his job. Robin's intuition, in fact, was right. Here was a weak link in the chain.

'Sammy, have you thought about it? Like I said?'

'Clam up, you. Remember, can't you, what I hand out when you get saucy-like?'

'Yes, I remember, all right. But when this is over I'll forget about it, Sammy. For your sake. I kind of like you, Sammy—although you're a rotten cook.'

'Cooking's dames' work. And you'll be down to dog biscuits—the three of you—if you don't clam up. Or puppy meal for the kid.' Sammy produced an uneasy chuckle at his own witticism. 'And that only in my own good time. This is just a routine visit, like. To see if those knots need a turn on them.'

'They don't—so it will be wasted effort. Listen, Sammy. Listen again. They go away, don't they, for hours at a time? So it's quite safe. And what do you get out of it all, anyway? Puppy meal, pretty well. They don't think much of you, Sammy. No respect.'

'It's none of your business, Master Bloody Upper-Class. Clam up, I say.'

'Okay, Sammy. Another time, perhaps. No hurry. Or is there?'

'What you mean—is there?'

'They may make their next move at any time, mayn't they? Fob you off with a few fivers, and perhaps a kick up the arse as well. When it might be thousands.'

'What you mean—thousands?' There was now distinguishable uncertainty in Sammy's voice.

'I've told you, haven't I? By this time there's sure to be a big reward out. Just for a quiet tip-off they'll pay it—believe you me. And see you safe to wherever you want to go. The States, Sammy. Chicago, say. There's real scope for a man of your wits in Chicago.'

'I'm loyal, I am.'

'You're a bloody liar there, Sammy. That's crap, and you know it. Treated you like dirt often enough, haven't they?'

'They fucking have.'

'Okay. Wait only till there's a clear couple of hours again. Untie these ropes, leave that door open, and make off to the nearest police station. You'll be safe as houses the moment you're with the pigs. You dictate something and sign it—for that's their drill—and those thousands are in your pocket in no time. They'll come straight from the Queen.'

There was a brief silence, in which I had the anxious thought that with that last stroke Robin had perhaps overplayed his hand. Sammy was certainly no genius. But that bit about the Queen was surely treating him as pretty well E.S.N.

'I'll think,' Sammy muttered. The torch went out. The door banged. He was gone.

'That takes us just a little further.' Robin's voice, only moments before strong and confident, suddenly owned utter exhaustion. 'I'd close for a dog biscuit like a shot,' he said.

# XV

I DON'T INTEND to enlarge on the later course of our captivity or the severe discomforts it imposed upon us. It had its phases or stages. Only Sammy ever appeared, although we heard the voices of our more important tyrants from time to time. Occasionally Robin went to work on him again. More frequently—and I thought with remarkable judgement—he left his subversive ideas to incubate slowly in Sammy's dim mind. There were small physical ameliorations now and then, and some sudden brutalities as well. Whether I bore myself well or ill, I don't know; what I can alone recall with any satisfaction was eventually coaxing the terrified little Daviot into speech. It was a sufficiently slender achievement, but it brought to all three of us in some obscure way a considerable measure of relief. I suppose we differed one from another in our private fears. My own concerned the likelihood (failing a successful suborning of Sammy) of protracted stalemate in the situation, and our captors, although not run to earth, coming to realize that the other side wouldn't play; that letting convicts out of gaol simply wasn't on. They wouldn't kill us, since to do so would increase the penalties attending ultimate disaster if it came to them, and would be without any practical advantage meantime. Nor would they liberate us, since that would too quickly give away too much. *They would simply quit.* We'd hear some powerful car departing, and that would be that. My last days and hours would be like those of Ugolino and his sons in their dungeon.

There was an element of muddled thinking in this, which my circumstances might perhaps excuse. When I thought about Robin's thinking I saw no muddle at all. At first I questioned the wisdom of one condition he consistently sought to impose in his palaverings with Sammy. Sammy was to free us from our bonds and leave an unlocked door behind him before departing to seek the security and sadly imaginary reward awaiting him in that police station. But then I saw how significantly it would be a constraining of the dull-witted creature to a sense that he had burnt his boats behind him. On his way to that citadel of law and order he was only too likely to lose his nerve and hurry back to restore the *status quo*. But once he had left three freed prisoners behind him his only policy would be to make his own virtuous appearance among the police before we walked in on them ourselves. Once more there was a hazard of judging Sammy to be even more thick-headed than he was. It was sound psychology on Robin's part, all the same.

And it worked. On what was my own third day in the place, it worked. Only it didn't work quite as we might have hoped.

The powerful car did depart. But it did that regularly, Robin said, once, or sometimes twice, a day. We had no expectation that anything dramatic would follow. Our minds, I think, were working slowly by this time—and how weakened and stiffened were our limbs we had hitherto known only when, cautiously one at a time and for humble purposes, Sammy had partly undone our fetters.

Now, perhaps half an hour after his bosses had driven away, he did the whole job. Or we thought he'd done that, although later a small but awkward snag was to appear. He said not a word, and he worked still almost in darkness. We said not a word either—feeling, I suppose, that it might be the wrong word if we uttered it. The whole thing was like a criminal deed. Sammy clearly felt that way: that here at last he was committing a thoroughly immoral act. David, I imagine, scarcely thought at all. But with both Robin and myself Sammy's state of mind was catching. We were guilty men. This extraordinary fact of mind appears worth reporting.

Sammy crept away, still without a word. He left a chink of light behind him, so we knew we weren't locked in again after all. Robin insisted on our letting some ten minutes pass; if Sammy saw us hard upon his heels, he said, he might imagine we were intent on double-crossing him—and it was just possible that he was lethally armed and might utterly lose his head. He had lost most of it already, or he would never have permitted this extraordinary state of affairs. It will be clear that, by this time, I was as entirely in Robin Hayes's hands as David Daviot was. Robin, for weeks now Heynoe's problem pupil, had taken command of our situation to quite staggering effect.

Staggering in the more literal sense now turned out to be the condition of all three of us. Gropingly, holding out a steadying hand each to the other, we stumbled out of the half-light of our prison without a glance at it. There was a narrow corridor, fabricated out of breeze-blocks and lit by two broken windows. Beyond this, we were in a very large, low-ceilinged room in which were a few pieces of furniture and some utensils—a cooking-stove, a camp bed, two or three kitchen chairs and the like—but which was mostly given over to bits and pieces of broken and rusted machinery. There was something queer about the daylight, which seemed to come mostly from the dirty roof over our heads. It was our long spell in almost utter darkness, I told myself, that had somehow disordered our vision. But at least before us was an open door, and one giving on open air. Strength came to us to run—uttering, I seem to remember, senseless cries. We were outside and in a free universe. It was a universe of snow.

Under a dull grey sky the snow was everywhere. It topped and sheathed and almost obliterated an endless disorganized huddle of derelict and crumbling and long-deserted buildings. Although the entire forlorn and sinister scene was swimming before me I recognized it at once. It was Uptoncester's luckless and ruined industrial estate. And we were as alone in it as if we had been pitched down on the surface of the moon.

But it was only for a moment that this impression, reassuring, even comforting after a fashion, held. There were four figures at a middle distance, and some way beyond them, barely visible through falling and eddying snow, was a large car, stationary and slanted sideways on what must have been a road. It appeared to have slewed or skidded on the treacherous surface and bumped into a wall. The four men were plodding in our direction. Their movement suggested a slow menacing ritual dance of savages as step by step they extricated their feet from what must have been eighteen inches of snow. I remembered that bit about there not having been such a winter for years.

They were the enemy. We hadn't a doubt of that. They were the enemy, who had for some reason been making an untimely return to their private prison. It occurred to me to wonder whether they had come upon Sammy, and dealt with him, on their way. Certainly they were going to deal with us now. There wasn't a doubt of that either. Even as we looked, aghast, they had spotted us. Faintly through the muffling downpour there came to us what must have been an enraged bellow. The oncoming dance turned energetic, phrenetic. They looked to be powerful men. It was unsurprising that Sammy was dead scared of them.

'*Run!*'

This was Robin's shout, and we ran. We ran in the only direction open to us, although it was probably clean away from Uptoncester and into a void and friendless countryside. Within a minute I was finding it difficult to keep up with the boys, and this puzzled me. Though elderly, I knew myself to be in reasonably fit physical trim. Then the explanation appeared. I wasn't running but hobbling. I was hobbling because, still tied firmly round one ankle, was a trailing length of Sammy's accursed rope. Quite how this impeded me, I don't know. But trying to cope with it as I moved, I came an abrupt cropper in the snow. There ought to have been nothing fatal about this, and I picked myself up in a moment. But now something nasty had happened to the ankle itself, and I lost further ground on Robin and David. Correspondingly, our pursuers gained upon me. I wondered whether I could effectively delay them by turning and putting up a fight. But it certainly wouldn't need four men to dispose of me as their fancy took them, and two of them would probably be enough to recapture the boys.

I was still wondering about this, weighing the possibility of a rugger tackle, when all four men came abreast of me and laboured on without a pause. I just mightn't have been there. They weren't interested in the intrusive schoolmaster—or an insignificant snooping cop. Their original captives, the only important ones, were still ahead.

I remembered what lay immediately in front of us all: the enormous gravel pit which had been turned, with small success, into an Aquatic Leisure Park. Nobody was going to be leisured there now. I wondered whether the great expanse of dirty water was frozen over—and, if so, whether it would also be under a blanket of snow.

Then, with amazing suddenness, the entire situation was transformed.

The sound of an engine made itself heard behind us. Then the sound of many engines. It was as if a whole traffic jam had dropped out of the sky upon this empty terrain. Labouring uselessly in the rear of the desperate chase, I halted and looked behind me. There was a police car, now stationary, not a hundred yards away. There were more police cars following, and in an instant policemen were tumbling out of the whole lot. As if by way of variety, there was also what I thought of as a Black Maria, and a couple of men were tumbling out of that too. Closing the amazing procession was an ambulance. Its bell was clanging violently—possibly by way of intimating to the criminals that all was up with them, and that they would presently be inside it and in poor condition if they resisted arrest.

But the race went on regardless. David was out in front. Perhaps because lighter than Robin, and so sinking less heavily into the snow as he ran, he looked to be the first who would breast some imaginary tape. The four pursuers were in a clump together, but must have been by now conscious that they were themselves pursued.

'*Stop, David! Stop!*'

It was Robin's shout again. Robin, having become aware as David had not of the transformed state of the case, knew that flight was no longer required of either of them. They had only to stand their ground and the police would be up with them almost in the same moment as with the enemy. An Uptoncester boy, he also knew about the gravel pit—the gravel pit in which it had been possible to water-ski or to indulge in the fascinating new

*Planche à Voile.* The kidnappers knew about it too. Even as I looked, two of them turned one way and two of them the other, proposing to skirt the great sheet of ice—for it was that—on opposite banks. No longer hunters but hunted, their aim was simply to escape amid the obliterating snows if they could.

David, still in blind terror, paid no heed to Robin's cry. He ran straight ahead, and in an instant was in mortal danger. The snow his heels sent flying no longer covered solid earth. Beneath it was the ice—perhaps no more than a skin of ice—and beneath that again dark water of unknown depth. On this new surface the boy ought to have slipped and fallen almost at once. But for fatal seconds, for a score of paces, his balance held. Then disaster struck. The ice split beneath him with a sound like a pistol-shot, shattering into fragments for a wide space around. And the judge's grandson had disappeared.

It was now the police that shouted—commanding Robin to stop. But Robin didn't. He didn't pause for an instant. He was in the water amid jagged stars of floating ice. Then he too vanished. When he reappeared he had David in his grasp. There were policemen—some of the policemen—in the water as well. Heavy-booted, they had plunged straight in. Others of them continued to pursue the criminals. I had a weird brief glimpse of them vanishing from the picture with unnatural speed, as in some grotesque episode of knockabout comedy on a screen. Robin was struggling with David towards the shore. There were policemen, up to their necks in water, only yards away. Then what seemed the final horror happened. The rescue went wrong, for the rescuer had succumbed to panic—just as in the Helmingham swimming bath on a day that seemed aeons remote. In a flailing confusion, both boys vanished.

There was a strange cry, and a new figure dashed past me. I recognized him as one of the men who had jumped from the Black Maria. I recognized, in fact, Robin's father: Mr Hayes, that talented escapologist. He was in the water—and as a professional among amateurs. None of the policemen now gallantly floundering had ever played water polo and gained a half-blue for it. They did their job, all the same—receiving first one and then the other boy into strong supporting arms. His effort made, Mr Hayes himself was only a few strokes from shore. But suddenly he gave another, and yet stranger, cry. His head went under. It didn't come up again. Perhaps his heart was dicky. Perhaps even, he'd had enough: one simply doesn't know. When they recovered his body it was to be under thicker ice near the middle of the pool.

Surprisingly, I found that Owen Marchmont was standing beside me.

'How on earth . . .?' I asked.

'That chap Ogilvy's work. Smart fellow for a desk-wallah. Found a pal of one of the men in gaol—Kissack—had operated, and still seemed to own, some crack-pot concern in this—heaven save us—industrial estate. It was a lead. Then there turned out to be a council employee who patrols it once a week, and who had spotted some odd activities. It struck Ogilvy as worth piling in. As for the old sod, I thought to come over and pick him up quietly from the family home myself. The police van was to accommodate the real crooks as well.'

'You wouldn't call Hayes a real crook?'

'He was a bloody small one. But I always thought there was some spunk in him.' Marchmont said this with satisfaction. 'And now he's quit of another open prison.'

I didn't much attend to this last philosophical remark. I was looking at the two survivors, stripped of their sodden clothes and huddled in warm blankets from the ambulance in which they would presently be carried away, certified as suffering from 'shock'. Now they were sitting side by side on a bench, staring blankly ahead, unaware of one another. Robin seemed older, and his physical likeness to his dead father had increased oddly. David, barbarously bereft of his golden curls, had a head too small for his body. He had become rather an unattractive boy.

ST  Stewart, J. I. M.

An open prison.